MEET THE GIRL TALK CHARACTERS

Sabrina Wells is petite, with curly auburn hair, sparkling hazel eyes, and a bubbly personality. Sabrina loves magazines, shopping, sleepovers, and most of all, she loves talking to her best friends.

Katie Campbell is a straight-A student and super athlete. With her blond hair, blue eyes, and matching clothes, she's everyone's idea of little miss perfect. But Katie has a few surprises for everyone, including herself!

Randy Zak has just moved to Acorn Falls from New York City, and is she ever cool! With her radical spiked haircut and her hip New York clothes, Randy teaches everyone just how much fun it is to be different.

Allison Cloud is a Native American Indian. Allison's super-smart and really beautiful. But she has one major problem: She's thirteen years old, five foot seven, and still growing!

Here's what they're talking about in
Girl Talk

RANDY: Hi, Al. I called to find out how your tutoring session with Billy went this afternoon.

ALLISON: Okay, I guess.

RANDY: Just okay? Hey that dude didn't give you a hard time, did he?

ALLISON: No, but I think I've just complicated things.

RANDY: Why do you think that?

ALLISON: Well, I've just invited him over to my house after school on Thursday to study!

FALLING IN LIKE

By L. E. Blair

GIRL TALK® series created by Western Publishing Company, Inc.

Produced by Angel Entertainment, Inc.

Western Publishing Company, Inc., Racine, Wisconsin 53404

Library of Congress Catalog Card Number: 90-84540 ISBN: :0-307-22010-9   B C D E F G H I J K L M

Text by Naomi Wolfensohn

Chapter One

"Hi, Allison! Did you find out who you're tutoring yet?" Katie Campbell, one of my best friends, asked as she sat down beside me at the lunch table. She pulled off her big, grey Bradley Junior High ice hockey sweatshirt. Then she straightened her pale pink turtleneck and smoothed her long blond hair. My friends and I all go to Bradley Junior High School.

"Yeah, who is she?" asked Sabrina Wells, another one of my best friends. She straightened the neon-green comb that was falling out of her long curly red hair. "I think it's awesome that you're doing this, Al," Sabs continued. I noticed that the comb matched her green jumper exactly. Sabs is very fashion conscious and into wearing the trendiest clothes and styles. I'm a little more conservative myself.

"What's awesome?" Randy Zak, my third best friend, wanted to know as she sat down next to me. She had a container of strawberry yogurt in one hand and her Walkman in the other. Randy was wearing a black knee-length T-shirt over black leggings. The T-shirt had a big white peace symbol on the front. Her black high-top sneakers, white socks, and silver peace symbol earring completed her outfit. Black happens to be Randy's favorite color. Of the four of us, she's the wildest dresser. Maybe it has to do with the fact that she's from New York City and only moved here to Acorn Falls, Minnesota, this year after her parents got divorced.

"The peer tutoring program," I replied, brushing my long black braid over my shoulder. "It's a program where kids from Bradley tutor other kids who are having trouble with some of their classes." It was called cooperative learning, or something like that and Ms. Staats, our English teacher who also happens to be my favorite, had suggested I do it. So I had gone to the informational meeting last week and I had decided that it sounded like a really good idea.

"So, Al, out with it," Sabs demanded, practically bouncing in her seat. "Who are you tutoring? Who is she?" That's one thing I love about

Sabs. She gets excited about everything and she always has to know exactly what's going on all the time. It's funny that we're friends because we're so different. I'm a lot quieter and I love to read and write poetry.

"She is a he," I replied softly. I already knew how Sabs was going to react. And she did.

"You're tutoring a boy!?" she exclaimed. "That's wild! I should have been a tutor."

"So, who is he?" Randy wanted to know, spooning up the last of her yogurt.

"I don't know him," I told Randy. Secretly, I felt a little nervous. I think not knowing who the person was made me even more nervous. And it wasn't because I was going to be tutoring a boy. After all, I was used to hanging out with Sabrina's twin brother, Sam, and his friends, so why was I nervous about someone I hadn't even met?

"Okay, Allison, please tell us," Katie put in, her blue eyes serious. Katie doesn't talk a lot so we're kind of alike in that way. But she surprised all of us earlier this year when she did something I could never imagine doing in a million years — she joined the boys' ice hockey team.

3

"His name is Billy Dixon," I finally said. "I don't think he's in any of my classes. Anyway, Ms. Staats says he's behind in almost every subject. I'm supposed to meet him after school today and . . . "

I let my voice trail off because I noticed that my three best friends were just sitting there staring at me with their mouths open. "What's wrong?" I asked them.

"I knew it," Sabs said with a heavy sigh. "I knew I should have signed up to be a tutor." She pulled a handful of carrot sticks out of her lunch bag.

"What luck," Katie said, smiling at me. "It sounds like fun. Besides, Billy is really cute — and tall." I think she added that part about his height because I'm one of the tallest girls in the seventh grade.

"So you guys know him?" I asked, suddenly feeling a little less nervous. I realized I would feel whole lot calmer if I knew something about this boy. "What's he like?"

"I've heard of him," said Randy. "I also heard he's really cool," Then she added, "for Acorn Falls." She smiled at all of us to let us know that she was only kidding. We all knew that Acorn Falls was really beginning to grow on her. "Well, he's got great blue-grey eyes and dark brown hair —" Sabrina began enthusiastically.

Katie, Randy and I looked at each other and laughed.

"Sabs," Katie interrupted her, "I think Al wanted to know what he's like as a student, not what he looks like. "

"Oh," Sabs said, swallowing a bite of carrot. "Well, I do know that his mother died of cancer, I think, about five years ago. He and his two brothers live with their father —"

Suddenly, there was a loud crash at the other end of the cafeteria. Everyone turned around to see what had happened. A tall boy in a brown leather bomber jacket was standing near the cashier's table at the end of the lunch line. He was holding a shorter boy — an eighth grader named Eliot Barrett — by the shoulders and shaking him. An entire tray of food was splattered across the floor at their feet.

"Watch where you're going!" the taller boy yelled suddenly.

"But you bumped into me," Eliot protested.

"Right, four eyes," the tall boy sneered,

pointing at Eliot's glasses. "You're the one who can't see, not me. Now, are you going to clean this up and buy me another lunch, or . . . " He trailed off as if he didn't even have to voice the threat.

"But I didn't —" Eliot tried again.

"I've had enough out of you, kid," the tall boy growled. "I'm going to give you one more chance —"

Mr. Grey, our social studies teacher, walked up behind them. "That's enough boys!" he shouted, putting a hand on each of their shoulders. "I want you both to come with me, right now!" He led them away, as a janitor walked out from the kitchen with a mop to clean up the mess.

"Phew!" Katie exclaimed, after we had all turned our attention away from the scene. "Does that answer your question, Al?"

"What do you mean?" I asked, confused.

"You wanted to know what Billy Dixon is like. Now you know," Randy replied.

I gulped. The tall, brown-haired, blue-eyed guy in the leather bomber jacket, the guy who had just made a big scene in the middle of the cafeteria — that was Billy Dixon!

"So he's a little pushy but I still think he's cool!" Sabrina practically gushed. "He's tall, and gorgeous and he hangs out with ninth graders —"

"Yeah, he's a definite dude," Randy commented. "Spike knows him. Billy actually went out with an eighth grade girl last year. Spike says he's cool, but kind of tough, you know what I mean?" she concluded, taking a sip of her orange juice and staring at me.

I could see what Randy meant after what had just happened between Billy and Eliot. Billy Dixon definitely had an attitude.

Now I was a nervous wreck. I thought peer tutoring was going to be a great experience. But Billy Dixon definitely did not seem like the kind of guy who would want my help. What had I gotten myself into?

Chapter Two

Did you ever notice how when you want to do something after school the day lasts forever, but when you're dreading something, the way I was, it flies by in a matter of minutes? Well, before I knew it, school was over.

I stood outside the door of Room 212 where Ms. Staats had said Billy would meet me. The door was closed, but I figured that he was already inside. Taking a deep breath, I tried to think of what I should say. I had thought about it the night before, but that was before I knew I was going to be tutoring Billy Dixon.

Then I thought about about how Billy had acted with Mr. Grey in the lunchroom. He hadn't looked scared at all, in fact, he had looked kind of bored. I realized that if a teacher didn't intimidate Billy, how could I? Billy was tough so I'd just have to be tough, too, in order to gain his respect.

8

Suddenly, I realized that I hadn't even *met* Billy Dixon and already I was imagining how awful he would be to work with. I gave myself a mental shake. I was going to march right in there and I was going to teach Billy whether he liked it or not. Taking a deep breath, I buttoned my red cardigan. I felt better like that — more official or something. I took one more deep breath to steady myself, and then I opened the door.

Billy was sitting with his feet up on a desk, his back toward the door, and he was staring out the window. His dark brown hair was slightly tousled, as if he had just run his fingers through it. He was wearing black jeans, a white T-shirt with the word "No" written on the back in black and black high top sneakers with the laces dangling. He was listening to his Walkman, and the music was so loud that I could hear it from across the room. No wonder he hadn't heard me come in.

For some reason, Billy reminded me of Randy, and the first time I had met her. She had been dressed all in black and was wearing a Walkman, too. But there was something else about Billy that reminded me of Randy — they both had an attitude as if they wanted to challenge you to a fight.

Randy is my absolute best friend. I understand her pretty well so I know that underneath all her toughness is a lot of vulnerability and pain. Looking at Billy, I realized that he might be just like Randy and that thought gave me the confidence to go in and do my best.

I put my books down on a desk behind Billy. Then I reached over and tapped him gently on the shoulder.

"Whoa!" Billy yelled and jumped out of his seat, ripping his Walkman off and whirling around to glare at me. "What did you do that for?" he demanded with a scowl.

"I didn't mean —" I began, taking a step backward. I really hadn't meant to startle him.

"Didn't anybody ever tell you not to sneak up on people like that?" Billy interrupted, still glaring at me. He had the most interesting eyes I had ever seen, kind of grey and blue at the same time.

"I'm sorry. I just —" I tried again.

"Who are you, anyway?" Billy asked suddenly, turning off his blaring Walkman. "What are you doing here?"

"I'm supposed to be here," I replied quickly. I figured it was the only way I would ever be able to say anything. "Ms. Staats told me—"

"Staats, huh," Billy commented knowingly. "Well, if you're here to get tutored, clear out. I'm supposed to meet my tutor here — not that I need one, or anything," he added quickly. "I had a choice between this tutoring thing and detention." He shrugged. "At least this'll be a change from detention."

"You don't understand," I said, my mind whirling. Had Billy been threatened with detention if he didn't agree to meet with me? The confidence I'd felt just a moment ago was beginning to melt. "I'm your tutor," I stated, my voice quavering. "My name is Allison Cloud and —"

"You're not old enough to be a teacher," Billy said accusingly. "How could you be my tutor? Now quit messing around and scram. I've got better things to do." Billy started to put back on his headphones.

"Wait!" I exclaimed. Billy stopped in mid-motion, raised one eyebrow and looked at me expectantly. "I really am your tutor," I said in a rush. "This is a peer tutoring program. All of the tutors are in the same grades as the students they're tutoring."

"That's weird," Billy replied, but he put his headphones down on the desk in front of him. "So, what are you supposed to teach me, Miss Brain?" he asked mockingly.

"Well . . . I . . . uh," I stuttered, thinking furiously. I hadn't expected him to just give in like that. "Math," I said finally, picking up a book from the pile I had brought in with me. I sat down quickly, and pulled out my math notebook. Maybe if I got right down to business, things would work out all right.

I took a deep breath. "Ms. Staats gave me a list of the subjects we're supposed to go over, so we'll start by multiplying fractions. " I opened my book, chose a problem, and began to write it out.

"You know, I haven't handed in an assignment in two weeks," Billy announced almost proudly. I didn't say anything. I stole a glance to my left, and saw that he had returned to his seat and was staring out the window again.

"I think that the easiest way to do these problems is to reduce the original numbers as much as you can," I began nervously. It was hard to concentrate on the math problem while Billy was sitting there silently with his back to me. But I was determined that he would learn something today — whether he liked it or not. I read the problem aloud, stumbling through the solution. "And the answer is eight thirty-fifths," I said at last.

"Wrong," Billy announced in a bored tone of voice.

"What did you say?" I asked quickly, shocked to find that he had been listening.

Billy turned around and faced me with a scornful, crooked sneer on his face. "I said," he replied, slowly and clearly, "that you are wrong. The answer is six thirty-fifths, not eight thirty-fifths."

Astonished, I looked down at my notebook and checked my work line by line. Somewhere along the way, I had lost a number. Billy was right! I stared at Billy, my mouth hanging open in surprise. How had he known that? He hadn't even looked at my paper, much less taken out his own notebook and done the problem himself. He must have done it in his head. I can't multiply fractions in *my* head, and I'm an A-student in math!

"What kind of tutor are you?" Billy asked. "You can't even do a simple math problem right," he laughed.

I was so embarrassed. I stared down at my paper and fought back tears. How could I have made such a stupid mistake?

"I told them I didn't need a tutor," Billy exclaimed, suddenly angry. He leaped up from his chair, strode to the front of the room and then whirled around to face me. "I can think circles around you know-it-all teacher's pets," he hissed, his eyes glinting like steel. "I've got enough people telling me what to do all the time, butting their noses into my life. I don't need some brain walking in here and trying to show me up."

Quietly, one tear rolled down my cheek and splashed on the math paper in front of me. I moved my hand to cover the wet spot, hoping that Billy hadn't noticed. "You know," Billy said with a harsh laugh, "I actually thought that junior high was going to be different. New teachers, different kids to hang around with . . . but it's no different. It's like they put this sign on you that only the teachers can see. And if the sign says A-student, then you get all A's, no matter what. And if the sign says troublemaker," he stopped and laughed again and a shiver crept up and down my spine at the sound of it. "If that's what it says," Billy went on, "well, then you might as well forget it, 'cause nobody cares and nobody ever will."

Another tear followed the first, falling on my hand. Out of the corner of my eye, I watched Billy walk back to where he had left his books and his jacket. Then I watched him cross the room, open the door, and slam it behind him.

I dug into my pocket for a tissue and wiped the tears from my face. I couldn't believe what a disaster this had turned out to be. Billy Dixon had frightened, confused, and embarrassed me and all I had managed to do was start crying. Well, I'm not going to let him do this to me again, I promised myself. I don't care if he does get left back next year . . . Suddenly, I heard Billy's last words ring through my head, "Nobody cares and nobody ever will."

It's not true, I said to myself. I do care whether Billy gets left back next year. Even though he had been totally obnoxious, there was something about Billy Dixon that drew me to him. I knew he was smart — I'd never met anyone who could multiply fractions in his head before. And if he was that smart, then there was no reason for him to be doing so badly in school.

Well, I'm not going to let him get away with it, I told myself firmly. I stood up and gathered my books together. I'm going to come back here tomorrow and be the best tutor that anyone has ever seen. That's one thing about me — I love challenges and I never give up. By the time I was through with him, Billy Dixon was going to pass seventh grade with flying colors!

Chapter Three

When I walked into Fitzie's a few minutes later, I saw Sabs, Katie, and Randy right away. They were sitting in our favorite booth at the back near the old-fashioned jukebox. All the other tables were full, but for once the aisles between the tables were clear. Since it was four o'clock, I figured that a lot of kids had gone home already. It was still pretty noisy, though.

"Hey, Al!" Sabs called when she saw me walking toward the table. "Did you hear? The student council is showing two movies at school next Friday night!"

"They're setting the gym up like a real movie theater," Katie added.

"And the first movie they're showing is *Nightmare on Elm Street*," Randy said. "Whoever picked that out has excellent taste."

"You can sign up to sell tickets or candy, or to be an usher," Sabs went on enthusiastically. "The only bad part is that Stacy Hansen is in charge because she's on the student council," Sabs then let out a big sigh. Stacy Hansen is blond, popular, and a flag girl. She also happens to be the principal's daughter. Something about this combination makes her sort of stuck-up, and for lots of reasons she's not too crazy about Sabs, Randy, Katie,and me.

Katie shuddered. "Can you imagine having Stacy boss you around all night?" she asked.

"That would be almost as bad as having Freddie come into your dreams," Randy commented. We all laughed. Freddie is the psychotic killer in the *Nightmare on Elm Street* movies. I had no idea who he was until I met Randy. She loves horror movies, and the gorier the better.

The waitress came by and I ordered a vanilla malted. Katie, Sabs, and Randy all ordered sundaes.

"How did your tutoring session go, Al?" Sabs asked.

"It was . . . um . . . okay," I answered quietly, focusing my eyes on my hands as I balled up a paper napkin. I really didn't feel like talking about it since I wasn't sure what to think about it myself yet.

Randy looked at me closely. "Just okay?"

she asked.

"Well, first I had to meet Billy," I began.

"By yourself?" Sabs asked.

I nodded. "Ms. Staats wants us to work together the first week without her interference. Then Billy and I will meet with her every two weeks after that."

"So, what did you say to him?" Katie asked.

"Well, he took one look at me and told me I was in the wrong room."

"He did?" Sabs asked, surprised. "What did you do then?"

"I told him who I was," I replied. "He didn't believe me when I explained that I was his tutor." As soon as I said that, I realized that more than anything else, I was mad at Billy Dixon. I was mad at him for being obnoxious to me for no reason and for not even trying to do his homework. My father is always saying that you have to work hard for what you want. I believe that.

"So, then what did you say?" Katie asked.

I shrugged. "I just took out my math book and told him that we should start to study. Then I mentioned something about him being behind in his classes. He told me he hasn't handed in an assignment in two weeks!"

"How does he get away with that?" Randy wanted to know. "The teachers at Bradley get on your case if you miss homework even once!"

"He didn't get away with it," Katie pointed out. "They gave him a tutor, didn't they?"

"Anyway," I went on, "I started going over the first math problem, but he wasn't paying attention. I got so frustrated that I made a mistake somewhere along the way, and Billy caught it!"

"Oh, no," Katie said.

"Oh, no, is right," I agreed. "Billy asked me how was I supposed to help him when I couldn't even get a simple math problem right. He got me so upset that I actually started to cry."

"Oh, Al, it sounds just awful," Sabs said sympathetically, her hazel eyes dark with concern.

"The next thing I knew, he left. And that was that," I finished.

"What a jerk," Sabs commented. "First he does everything he can to make you want to leave, and then he takes off as if it's all your fault, or something."

"Sounds like this guy has a major problem with reality," Randy added as the waitress brought over our order.

"Are you going to go back tomorrow?" Katie asked, spooning up some vanilla ice cream and strawberries.

"Yes, I am," I replied immediately.

"All right, Al," boomed Randy, slapping me hard on the back. "You're no quitter."

"That's right," I agreed. "Billy Dixon isn't going to turn me into a quitter. I just have to think of a way to get him to work with me."

Katie started giggling. "I could ask some of the guys from the hockey team to come with you and talk him into it," she suggested.

I pictured myself walking into Room 212 with the hockey team, all dressed in their pads and carrying their hockey sticks. I started laughing, too.

"He might be too scared to work," Sabs said with a giggle.

"Yeah," Randy put in, "Or, maybe he'd make himself sick by laughing too hard. Billy Dixon doesn't sound like the kind of guy who gets scared easily."

That was definitely true. I remembered the way Billy had yelled at Eliot in front of the whole cafeteria. I remembered how he hadn't even looked scared when Mr. Grey broke up their argument. There was no way I was going to try and force Billy to study.

"Why is he behind in so many of his classes, anyway?" Katie asked.

"He probably just hates school," Randy replied. "Spike told me that Kevin Dixon is always skipping classes and that he's even gotten suspended a few times. Kevin always says that he hates school, and he's going to quit as soon as he turns sixteen, like their older brother, Tom," she finished.

"I didn't know that," I said. I couldn't imagine hating school so much that I would want to quit. I think it's fun to learn new things all the time.

"Yeah," Sabs put in. She fished around in her sundae, trying to find the cherry. "I guess Billy Dixon is just like his older brothers."

"Well, one way or another I'm going to find out," I told Sabs. But then I thought about something Billy had said. I wondered what it would be like to go to school every day if all of my teachers expected me to do badly because of the way other kids in my family had done. I'd probably start hating school, too, no matter how much I liked learning.

"Hey, Al," Randy said, interrupting my thoughts. "If Billy Dixon hates school so much, why don't you try tutoring him somewhere else?"

"Like where?" Sabs asked curiously.

"I don't know," Randy replied, shrugging. "Why not here?"

"At Fitzie's?" I asked, not sure I had heard her right.

"At Fitzie's?" Katie repeated. "How could anybody get any studying done here? It's too noisy."

Randy shrugged. "I can't study when it's too quiet. I usually play one of the rock tapes my friend Sheck sends me from New York."

Sometimes it amazes me that Randy and I are so different. I mean, I can't study unless it's totally quiet. I usually sit in the window seat in my bedroom, where I can look out the window once in a while. It's so peaceful and comfortable there that it's easy for me to concentrate.

That's what Billy needs, I thought.

Someplace where he's comfortable enough to study. Someplace where he doesn't have to think about school. Just then, the most unlikely thought struck me. Maybe I should bring Billy home with me.

Suddenly, I shivered. Billy Dixon — at my house? I had to be crazy to even think about it! Still, I already knew that tutoring him at school wasn't going to work. Maybe I should try it. All I had to do was ask him.

"Ouch!" Sabrina yelled, breaking into my thoughts. "Cut it out, Sam!" She turned around and glared at her twin brother, Sam, while rubbing one hand on the back of her head. "I told you not to pull my hair anymore," she said.

"Oh, come on, Blabs," Sam said, a huge grin on his freckled face. "You know that didn't hurt."Sam's favorite nickname for Sabrina is Blabs because she likes to talk so much and so fast.

"Maybe it didn't hurt you," Sabs complained, "but I probably have a bald spot now. Why did I have to get stuck with four brothers?" She rolled her eyes.

"I guess you're just lucky little sister," Sam said, shrugging. Sam was born exactly four minutes before Sabrina, which makes her the youngest person in her family, as well as the only girl. Sam never lets her forget it either. Sabs and Sam are quite a pair. They both have red hair, hazel eyes and freckles, and they're both a lot of fun. They bicker a lot, but they love each other.

"Go away, Sam," Sabs said, making a shooing motion with her hand. "We're talking."

"Okay, okay. I'll leave," Sam sighed, dramatically. "I guess you'll just have to wait to hear my incredible news." He turned around and started to walk away.

I smiled. Sam knows better than anyone that Sabs can't stand knowing that someone else knows something that she doesn't.

"Wait!" Sabrina called after him. "What incredible news?"

"Oh, nothing," Sam teased. "I don't want to bother you if you're talking."

"Sam!" Katie joined in with Sabrina's pleas. "Please tell us."

"Well," Sam hesitated, a twinkle in his hazel eyes. "Okay." He came back and stood at the end of our table. "Remember the old bowling alley that closed down last summer? Lois

Lane's?"

"I remember," Katie said. "I used to go there a lot."

"Me, too," Sabs added. "What about it?"

"Nick just told me that some businessman from Minneapolis took it over, and it reopened last week!" Sam announced.

"Intense!" Randy exclaimed. "I love bowling. Sheck and I used to bowl all the time."

"We should definitely go," Sabs said, looking excited.

"Lois Lane's was really great before they closed it," Katie said. "Everybody used to have parties there and stuff. "

"You haven't heard the best part yet," Sam continued. "The owner wants people to start coming in again so he's running all kinds of specials. Bradley Junior High has a half-price deal on Friday from six to nine!"

"Awesome!" Sabrina exclaimed.

"So, what we were thinking — Nick, Jason, Greg and I — was that we guys could show you girls how it's really done," Sam finished

"What do you mean?" Sabs asked suspiciously, her eyes narrowing as she stared at her brother, and crossed her arms.

"I mean," Sam said with a grin, "we challenge you girls to a match — the guys against the girls. Of course, you don't have a chance, but it'll be fun anyway."

"You're on," Randy and Katie said together.

"What do you mean, we don't have a chance?" Sabs asked hotly. "We're gonna destroy you!"

"Yeah, right!" Greg Loggins said sarcastically, joining Sam at the end of the table. He shook his straight blond hair back from his face and stared at us obnoxiously. "Like you could *even* think about beating us!"

"Just you wait," Sabrina told him, her face flushing red.

"Hey!" Sam interrupted, laughing. "This is just supposed to be a friendly bowling match — not a fight to the death! Come on, Greg. Let's find Nick and Jason and go shoot some hoops. See you later, guys!"

"'Bye, Sam," we all called after him.

"I can't believe that Greg Loggins!" Sabs exclaimed after the guys had left Fitzie's. "He is so rude!"

Katie giggled. "I can still remember when you had a crush on him," she said.

"I did not," Sabrina denied, blushing.

"Yes, you did," I teased. "While we were on Eagle Mountain that time, Greg Loggins was the only thing you talked about!"

"Well, I don't like him now," Sabs told us firmly. "And I'm definitely going to beat him at Lois Lane's on Friday. "

"Um, guys," I said, hesitantly. "I don't know if I should go bowling with you on Friday."

"Why not?" Randy asked, sounding surprised.

"I've never gone bowling before," I told them. "I don't know how. Maybe you'd better ask somebody else to bowl with you —"

"Al! Don't be silly!" Katie interrupted me. "Bowling is easy and you'll pick it up just like that." She snapped her fingers.

"We'll help you," Sabrina offered.

"It'll be awesome," Randy assured me. "And I have this funny feeling that you'll turn out to be quite a bowler, Al," she concluded.

"It's getting kind of late, guys," Katie said suddenly, looking at her watch. "I'd better get home and start my homework." She stood up and grabbed her knapsack.

Sabs groaned. "Thanks for reminding me! I

promised Mom I'd help her make dinner tonight. I've got to get home fast!"

"Let's hit it," Randy said, swinging her black leather knapsack up onto her shoulder.

The four of us left Fitzie's and walked a few blocks together. Then we went our separate ways. I kept trying to think of some natural way to ask Billy Dixon over to my house for a tutoring session. I couldn't help wondering what was going to be harder: learning how to bowl or helping Billy Dixon. But it didn't really matter. I just had to try really hard to do both.

Chapter Four

During dinner that night my parents asked me all kinds of questions about tutoring. Even though I knew they were just interested and concerned, I felt sort of funny talking about it with them. There was something about Billy that I just couldn't put into words. I ended up telling them a little about Billy and how much I wanted to help him anyway.

"The first thing you have to do is let him know that you really care about what happens to him," my mother said, giving Charlie a second helping of mashed potatoes. "Then, when he trusts you, he'll let you start to help him." My mother used to be a teacher before my little brother Charlie and I were born. She said it sounded as if Billy needed a friend even more than a tutor.

I thought about what she said as I took a sip of water. "But how do I get him to trust me?" I asked. I couldn't imagine Billy trusting me. As it was, he was barely talking to me.

"Allison, I think you'll have to figure that part out for yourself," my mother said, smiling at me.

After dinner, I finished my homework, then curled up in my window seat with a book I was reading, *The Phantom Tollbooth*. It's one of my old favorites. It's the story of a boy named Milo who's incredibly bored with life. Then, somebody sends him into another world. Milo learns how important all the little things around him are — especially the things people take for granted, like sounds, words, numbers and the way the sun always rises in the East and sets in the West. As I climbed into bed, I wondered if Billy Dixon had ever read *The Phantom Tollbooth*.

The following day, Wednesday, I had to keep reminding myself that it was just an ordinary day. But all I could think about was Billy Dixon, and how I was going to ask him to come over to my house. I had trouble paying attention in class. The only thing that I remember really clearly is when Ms. Staats called me up to her desk at the end of homeroom.

"Allison," Ms. Staats began, "I hope everything went all right with your tutoring session yesterday? Oh," she went on, not even waiting for an answer, "before I forget, you won't be able to use Room 212 after school today. One of the teachers is giving a make-up test there. I've asked Billy to meet you in the library instead. Allison," Ms. Staats hesitated for a moment. "I know that you'll find it hard to work with Billy Dixon at times, but don't get discouraged. I chose you as his tutor for some very good reasons, and I'm confident that you'll do fine."

With that, Ms. Staats picked up her briefcase. "I have a parent-teacher conference this period," she told me, ushering me toward the door. "I'll see you tomorrow, Allison." Then she disappeared into the crowd in the hallway.

Before I knew it, it was three o'clock. I stopped by my locker to gather all the books I needed, and then went to the library to meet Billy. This time, I got there first.

I picked a table in a back corner of the room. It was sort of separated from the rest of the tables in the library by two huge bookcases. I took out my social studies book and started to read the chapter on the Colonization of

America. I was especially interested in reading about the Native Americans who had helped the first settlers in Plymouth, but there really wasn't too much about them. Besides, they couldn't have been Chippewa, which is what I am, because the Chippewa are a Midwestern tribe.

I got so involved in the reading that I didn't even notice that Billy had arrived until I heard his voice.

"Well, I'm here," he announced, loudly.

I looked up quickly. Billy was standing on the book ladder against the shelves behind me. I noticed that he was still wearing his leather bomber jacket. Underneath, he had on a black T-shirt and a pair of ripped, faded jeans.

"Good," I said firmly, determined that the two of us actually get some work done. I tried to push all thoughts of his obnoxious behavior of the day before out of my mind. "We have a test in social studies on Friday. I thought we could start by studying for that." There, I said to myself. I sounded as if I was in control and knew what I was doing.

Billy jumped down from the ladder and leaned against it, still smiling. I noticed again how tall he was. I may be tall, but even I have to look up a little bit to meet Billy's eyes. Having him stand so close to me was actually making me kind of nervous. "I already know all that stuff," he said confidently.

We'll see about that, I thought to myself, turning in my seat so that I was facing him. At least he was being a little less obnoxious then he had been the day before. Ms. Staats had told me that Billy had failed the last two tests in social studies. "Then, what year did the Pilgrims first land in America?" I asked him quickly.

"The Mayflower landed in December of 1620," Billy responded automatically.

"Where?" I asked, hoping to catch him.

"Cape Cod Bay," he replied, grinning. "They didn't hit Plymouth until after they decided that they didn't want to settle in Cape Cod."

I asked a few more questions and he answered all of them correctly. He really did know his social studies. "I guess we're finished with social studies then," I told him. "Just remember, Mr. Grey is probably going to ask us about Squanto, Samoset and Massasoit, too."

Billy moved a little closer to the table. "What are those?" he asked, scowling. "Grey didn't talk about them in class."

"Squanto, Samoset and Massasoit were some of the first Native Americans the Pilgrims met," I explained. I pointed to my book, open on the table in front of me. "It's in the reading."

Billy looked down at the book for a second. "I hate reading," he said shortly. "Let's do something else."

"Why do you hate reading?" I asked, staring at him.

"I just do," Billy interrupted me, shrugging. His voice sounded strange, almost as if he had a sore throat, and he wouldn't look at me.

I tried to imagine what it would be like to hate reading. I just couldn't do it. During the summer between sixth and seventh grades, I'd read over a hundred books — just for fun. Even now, I sometimes spend my study halls in the library, reading.

"Let's do math," Billy suggested, sitting down next to me at the table and pulling my math book out of the pile. He handed it to me.

"We should really finish going over the social studies if you haven't done all of it," I said disagreeing with him.

"Look, *Miss* Allison Cloud," Billy exclaimed. "Are you going to tutor me, or not?"

I nodded slowly.

"Then forget about that stupid social studies test and let's get going on the math!" Suddenly, he grinned. "It's been so long since I handed anything in to Old Lady Munson that I just know she's going to have a bird when I do."

I giggled, picturing Miss Munson sitting on a huge egg in the middle of her math class, shaking her finger at Billy. "Okay," I said, trying to keep a straight face. I opened my math book and read the first question aloud.

"A boy has one third as many apples as his brother does and one half the number of apples that his sister has. Together, all three children have eighteen apples. How many apples does each child have?" I looked at Billy. He was staring at something over my head, his forehead wrinkled. He looked as if he was confused about the problem, so I decided to explain it.

"First of all, you know that the boy has a certain number of apples," I began. "So you call *that* number of apples 'x' Then —"

"Three, six and nine," Billy said suddenly.

"What?" I asked, confused.

"The boy has three apples, his sister has six and his brother has nine," he repeated, a twinkle in his eyes. He leaned back in his chair. "Go ahead and check it. It's right."

Startled, I wrote the math problem out on a piece of looseleaf paper: $x+2x+3x=18$, so $6x=18$, so $x=3$. I looked at Billy in surprise. "You're right. I thought you said you haven't handed in any homework?"

"That's right," Billy replied.

"Then how did you get the answer so fast?" I asked.

"I just did it in my head," he told me, tapping the side of his head with his finger. "Math is easy."

"If it's easy then why don't you hand in your homework?" I questioned, suddenly feeling impatient. Ms. Staats had told me that Billy Dixon was in danger of failing seventh grade. Based on what I knew of him so far, it seemed to me that he should be getting all A's.

Billy waved his hand in the air. "It takes too long to write all that stuff down," he said. "I just do the problems in my head while Munson's going over them the long way." His grin got wider. "She doesn't know it, but I haven't made a mistake yet."

I looked at Billy, astounded. Was he telling the truth? Math isn't my favorite subject, but I'm usually good at it. Still, I would never be able to do the homework in my head. *Something really strange is going on here.* I thought to myself.

"You know," I said quietly, "the only way Miss Munson knows that you understand the material is if you hand something in."

"I already tried that," Billy said with a frown. "I wrote down all the answers and handed them in, just like everybody else. I got a zero every time. Munson told me to stop copying the answers from people and start doing my own work." He shrugged. "So I stopped handing stuff in."

"You just wrote down the answers all by themselves?" I asked. He nodded. "Miss Munson just wants to see your work," I told him. "She wants to know how you got the answer."

"But I got it by thinking it out," Billy said, sounding impatient. "Why should I have to write it down?"

"Because that's the way Miss Munson

wants us to do it," I said, knowing that it wasn't a very good reason.

"Yeah, well, I'm better at math than Old Lady Munson," Billy announced. "Who cares what she wants? Let's do something else." He leaned across the table and started looking through the rest of my books.

Confused, I tried to put everything I knew about Billy together so that it made some kind of sense. In the first place, he's on the verge of failing most of his classes. And he seems to hate school. He definitely hated reading. At the same time, he remembered almost everything Mr. Grey had told us about the Colonization of America in social studies and he could do math problems in his head three times faster than I could do them on paper. Whatever was going on, it was totally weird.

"Earth to Allison," Billy said quietly, interrupting my thoughts. "Come in, Allison."

"What?" I asked. I turned in his direction and almost gasped. He had leaned really close to me so that his face was only a few inches away from mine. I was so surprised to find him that close, I couldn't even blink.

Billy laughed and sat back. "I asked you if

we could get out of here. Some of my friends are waiting for me." He pushed back his chair and stood up.

"Billy, wait!" I said. He couldn't leave yet. I still hadn't asked him to come over to my house.

Billy rolled his eyes and sat back down. "Look, Allison," he began, "don't ask me to do the English reading or answer the science questions because I'm not going to do it. You just don't get it. Even if I liked school — which I don't — you couldn't get me to stay here. See, I'm just not cut out to be a brain."

"I think you're wrong," I told him quietly.

"Oh, yeah?" Billy sat back in his chair and folded his arms across his chest. He raised one eyebrow and looked at me with this cocky half smile on his face. "And why is that?"

"Because I already know that you're better at math than I am," I told him. "Maybe social studies, too. It's just that you need to work on your study habits." I hurried on before I lost my courage, keeping my fingers crossed for luck. "And I think the first thing you have to do is find some place where you can study comfortably. That's why I think we should meet at my house tomorrow after school," I finished in a rush. I couldn't believe it. I had actually invited him to my house.

For a minute, neither of us said anything. Billy just sat there with that sarcastic half-smile on his face. Then he stood up. My heart sank. He obviously did not want to come to my house. It had been a dumb idea.

"Where do you live?" Billy asked suddenly.

"Spencer Avenue," I answered automatically. "Number 42."

"I'll be there," Billy said. Then he turned and walked out of the library.

I watched him go, then heaved a deep sigh of relief. I was exhausted. Keeping up with Billy Dixon was even harder than keeping up with my little brother Charlie when he was in the mood to get into trouble. I also had a major case of butterflies in my stomach — the same kind of butterflies I had felt when this guy I sort of liked offered me a ride home from the *Belle Magazine* modeling session we were both in. His name was Moose, and he was really nice. But somehow the butterflies I felt now were worse. Maybe it was because this time, I had been the one to do the asking.

Chapter Five

"Mom! I'm home," I called as I walked into my house after school the next day. I sniffed the air. Mom was baking peanut butter cookies and the whole house smelled great.

"Hi, honey," Mom replied from the kitchen. "Come have a cookie. I just took them out of the oven."

I hung up my coat in the hall closet, dropped my knapsack next to the closet door, and went into the kitchen. "Did you see Charlie outside?" my mother asked.

"He's playing in the yard," I replied. Charlie is seven years old, and he's really into cartoon heroes. When I saw him, he was dressed all in green with a green plastic garbage can lid tied onto his back. He was pretending to be a Ninja Turtle.

"Is Billy still coming over?" my mother asked.

"I think so," I told her, pulling a stool up to

the counter and sitting down.

"When he does come, why don't the two of you work in the dining room," my mother suggested, handing me a warm cookie. "I'll keep Charlie out of your way."

"Thanks, Mom," I said gratefully. Just then, the doorbell rang. "I'll get it. " I jumped off the stool and practically flew to the front door. When I reached it, I stopped for a second to take a deep breath and try to overcome the butterflies in my stomach.

When I opened the door, Billy was leaning against the door frame with one foot crossed behind the other. The first thing I noticed was that he looked almost as nervous as I felt. Then, when he saw that it was me, he smiled. He was wearing his leather jacket, baggy bleached-out jeans and a bright blue sweatshirt that brought out the blue in his eyes.

"Well, I'm here," he announced, just the way he had said it at the library the day before. Hearing his voice made my stomach jump a little.

"Come in," I said as normally as I could.

"Is that your little brother in the yard?" Billy asked me as he stepped inside. "He said his name is Charlie."

"Yes, he's my brother. He's only seven and he can be sort of a brat sometimes," I told him.

"I like him," Billy told me. He held up a black knapsack. "So, where are we working?"

"In the dining room. It's right over here," I picked up my own knapsack and led Billy into the dining room. We sat down at the table.

"Is this where you study?" Billy asked, looking around. The wooden floor and dark, wood paneled walls of our dining room make it sort of formal, but my mom fills it with ferns and fresh flowers, straw baskets and light colored wall hangings, to brighten it up.

"Sometimes. But most of the time I go upstairs to my room. I have a window seat up there, and it's really quiet and comfortable."

"That sounds cool," Billy said with a grin. "I've always wondered if window seats were comfortable."

I smiled back. "It's important to study some place where it's quiet and you feel comfortable. At least, that's what my mother says. She was a teacher before I was born."

Billy just nodded.

"I thought we'd start with math," I said,

taking my math book and some paper out of my knapsack. "Since you need to show your work, why don't you tell me how you figure the problem out and I'll write down what you say."

Billy looked confused. "You mean, talk out loud while I solve the problem? I don't know if I can do that."

"Just try it," I encouraged him. "Here's the first one: Four businesses share the entire market for one product. Business A has three times the market share that Business B has, Business C has one half the market share that business A has and Business D has one and a half times the market share of Business A. What percentage of the market does each business have?"

For a second, Billy got the same faraway look in his eyes that he had had the day before

"Billy, tell me how you solve it," I said, softly.

His brow furrowed in concentration, Billy hesitantly started to speak. "All the businesses together have one hundred percent of the market, so that's how much the total is." He went on, describing the process to set up and solve the equation, while I wrote down what he said. "Business A has thirty percent, Business B has ten percent, Business C has fifteen percent and Business D has forty five percent," he concluded, brushing a lock of dark brown hair out of his eyes and looking at me triumphantly.

"Great!" I exclaimed, holding up the paper on which I had written Billy's solution. "That's exactly right."

"Phew!" Billy sighed. "It takes so much longer to say it than it does to just do it," he complained.

"I know. But at least you'll be able to hand in your homework tomorrow," I reminded him. "Let's do the next one."

Twenty minutes later, we finished the last of the eight word problems. Billy hadn't missed a single one. "There," I said, handing him the paper. "Now all you have to do is copy it over."

"Thanks," Billy said. He folded the page a couple of times and put it in the inside pocket of his jacket. Then he started laughing. "I can't wait to see old Miss Munson's face when she gets a look at this!"

I laughed along with him. His laugh was kind of loud and happy. I liked it — and I liked seeing him laugh. He let his guard down when he laughed and his eyes got all crinkly in the corners.

"What's next?" he asked, after we had caught our breath.

"English," I answered firmly, preparing myself for a storm.

"No way!" Billy said, just as firmly.

"Allison?" my mother called from the kitchen. "Do you and Billy want to take a break for a minute? I just took some more cookies out of the oven."

Billy laughed. "Saved by the bell," he joked. "Come on, let's take a break. I'm starving," he pleaded, standing up.

"Well," I began, pretending to hesitate. "I guess it's okay. But only if you promise to work on English afterwards."

"Maybe," Billy said as we walked into the kitchen, grinning mischievously.

"Mom, this is Billy Dixon," I introduced him. "Billy, this is my mother."

"Hello, Billy," my mother said, holding out a plate of cookies.

"Hi, Mrs. Cloud," he replied. "Thanks for the cookies."

"Why don't you pour a couple of glasses of milk, Allison," my mother suggested. "How's the studying going?" she asked Billy.

"Not bad," he told her. "Allison's a great teacher. " He looked at me and winked as I handed him a glass of milk.

"Good," my mother said. "Then take a few more cookies and get back to work." She ushered us out of the kitchen and back into the dining room.

Billy and I sat at the dining room table. I put my cookies and milk next to me and reached for our English book. Billy groaned.

"At least let me finish eating," he said. "Maybe by then it'll be time for me to go."

I laughed. "Why do you keep trying to get out of doing English?"

"Because I'm no good at it," he retorted with a frown.

"I am," a familiar voice suddenly said from out of nowhere. "I'm the best in my whole class!"

"Charlie?" I asked, looking around the room. I had definitely heard Charlie's voice, but I couldn't see him anywhere. "Where are you?"

"Here," Charlie answered, crawling out from under the table. "Mommy said you were studying with Billy. I want to study with Billy, too." Charlie held out a book.

"I thought Mom told you to leave us alone, Charlie —" I began.

"But I want to study with Billy!" Charlie complained loudly.

I looked hopelessly at Billy. Sometimes it's totally useless to say 'no' to Charlie. And before I could say anything else, Charlie climbed into the chair next to Billy and opened up his book.

"'Terry and Patty are friends. They like to play together.'" Charlie read.

Billy looked at me over Charlie's head. I just shook my head and shrugged. Billy opened his mouth and shut it. Then he turned his attention back to Charlie. I still hadn't figured Billy out. Was he really the same person I had seen in the cafeteria that day fighting with Eliot Barret? Because here he was now, listening to my seven-year-old brother read aloud as if it were the most interesting thing in the world. At least the story was sort of cute. Charlie and I had already read it together three or four times.

"What's this word, Billy?" Charlie asked suddenly. Billy, frowning, looked more closely at the book. I saw his lips moving.

"Can't *you* figure it out?" he asked Charlie

after a few seconds.

"I don't know that word yet," Charlie said. "You have to tell me what it is."

Billy looked at the page one more time. "Dolls," he said finally. "That's what it is. Dolls."

Charlie started again at the beginning of the sentence again. "'Patty and Terry take turns playing with their dolls.'" He looked up at Billy with a puzzled expression on his face. "I don't think Terry plays with dolls," he said. "Terry is a boy."

"Boys play with dolls, too, Charlie," I put in. Charlie must have found a new book about Terry and Patty. The story Charlie and I had read hadn't been about dolls.

"No, they don't," Charlie insisted. "Boys play with footballs and video games, right, Billy?"

Billy glanced over at me and then back to Charlie. "I think you'd better listen to your sister on this one," he advised, chuckling. "Read me the next sentence, okay?"

"'Patty took the ball away from Terry,'" Charlie read. "'Terry did not like that at all. He was . . .'" Charlie stopped reading and pointed to another word. "What does that say, Billy?" he asked.

Billy looked at the word Charlie was pointing out. "Annoyed," he said.

"'Terry was annoyed,'" Charlie read.

Annoyed? That was an awfully big word for one of Charlie's books. "Are you sure that's the right word?" I asked Billy quietly.

"Shh!" Charlie said, holding one finger to his lips. "I'm reading!"

Charlie continued to read without any problems until he reached the last page. "I don't know this word," he said, holding the book up to Billy's face.

"Ask Allison this time," Billy suggested, pushing the book away.

"But I want *you* to help me," Charlie insisted.

Billy sighed and took the book from Charlie. He looked at it for a second and then handed it back. "Close," he said shortly.

"'Terry and Patty are close friends. The End.'" Charlie read.

"Wait a minute, Charlie," I said. I knew from listening to the rest that this was definitely the same book I had read with Charlie before and I knew that that was not the right ending. I took the book from him and read the last page aloud. "'Terry and Patty are best friends. The End.' It's best, Billy, not close," I said quietly. "I think you read it wrong."

Billy stood up. "I told you I wasn't any good at English," he said angrily. "Listen, I don't have any more time for this tutoring stuff today. I've gotta go." He picked up his knapsack and slung it over one shoulder.

"But, Billy, we haven't —" I began.

"See you around," he cut in coldly. "Bye Charlie," he added, tousling my little brother's hair. Billy turned on his heel and walked out of the dining room.

"I like Billy," Charlie said, taking one of the peanut butter cookies that Billy had left behind.

"Me, too," I said.

"How come he was so mad?" Charlie asked, his mouth full of cookie crumbs.

"Don't talk with your mouth full, Charlie," I said automatically. I realized that I hadn't answered Charlie's question, but that was only because I was too busy trying to figure out the answer for myself. Why had Billy gotten so angry all of a sudden? All I had done was correct his reading. I reached across the table and pulled the book toward me. I read the last page again. Terry and Patty are best friends. The End. Were Billy and I still friends at all, I wondered.

Just then, my mother came into the dining room. "There you are, Charlie! I thought I told you to leave Billy and Allison alone," she scolded. She looked around. "Where is Billy? I was going to ask him if he wanted to stay for dinner."

"He went home," I told her. "I think he was mad about something."

"Oh?" Mom said, sitting down at the table with me. "What was he mad about? Did Charlie bother him?"

"No, Charlie was fine," I assured her. "He just came in and asked Billy to help him read a book." I explained how Billy had been helping Charlie, and that Billy had read the wrong word a few times. "When I corrected him the last time he got upset and left. And I wasn't mean about it, or anything."

"I'm sure you weren't," Mom replied, smiling. "What kind of mistakes was he making?" she asked.

I wrote down all the words on a piece of paper. Billy had read *dolls* instead of *toys*, *annoyed* instead of *angry* and *close* instead of *best*. My mother read over the list, then looked at me.

"Has Billy ever been tested for a reading disorder?" she asked seriously.

"A reading disorder?" I said, surprised. "I don't know. Why?"

"Well, there's almost a pattern in the mistakes that Billy made," Mom pointed out. "Look. The words he read have pretty much the same meanings in those sentences as the words that were actually there. That's the kind of thing that happens to a person who has a reading disorder."

"Does that mean that Billy will never be able to read?" I asked, curious.

"Well, we won't know if Billy has a reading disorder until after he's been tested," my mother said, shaking her head. "If he does, then it probably means that he'll have to be retrained. Only this time he'll learn how to read the right way."

"So, what should I do?" I asked.

"Why don't you talk to the teacher who

started the tutoring program," Mom suggested. "She'll probably know how to set up testing for Billy."

"I'll talk to Ms. Staats tomorrow," I agreed.

"Allison," Charlie said, walking over to stand beside me. "Is Billy going to come back and read with me again?"

"I hope so, Charlie," I replied, smiling. But I wasn't so sure how someone like Billy would react to the fact that he might have a reading problem. He was already mad at me. This might only make him angrier.

Chapter Six

I never got to speak to Ms. Staats on Friday. She had gone to a language convention in Minneapolis. I decided to go the library and look up reading disorders. I wanted to make sure I knew what I was talking about.

In the school library I found a huge, thick book called *Teaching Reading: Strategies and Stumbling Blocks*. The language in it was so difficult that I could barely read the table of contents. The only other thing I could find was an article in an encyclopedia, but my mother had already told me everything that was in that. I made up my mind to go to the Acorn Falls Public Library over the weekend.

All day, Sabs, Katie, and Randy kept talking about the bowling match we were having at Lois Lane's that night. I was starting to get nervous about it myself. At 6:15, we walked into the bowling alley. "This is intense!" Randy exclaimed. "I feel like I'm back in New York."

"We have some cool things in Minnesota, too, Ran, you know," Sabs told her proudly.

It did look pretty amazing. The whole place was decorated Fifties-style with a snack bar that looked like a Fifties diner, an old-fashioned jukebox and black and white pictures of movie stars all over the walls. There was also an arcade with a ton of pinball machines and video games. There were so many Bradley Junior High kids there that it was like one big party.

"I'm so psyched this place reopened," Sabs exclaimed. "This will be so much fun! Hey, come on, guys. Let's get our shoes. Maybe we can have a warm-up game before the guys get here."

"Who needs a warm-up game?" Randy asked confidently as we walked to a counter near the bowling lanes. "Those guys don't have a prayer."

"We're going to whip them," Katie agreed. Then she turned to give the man behind the counter our shoe sizes.

"Actually, I think a warm-up game would be a good idea," I put in.

"Al, are you still worried about learning to bowl?" Sabs asked teasingly as we sat down on a bench to change into our bowling shoes. "It's easy!"

"You'll do great," Katie added.

"You know, I used to have a pair of these shoes," Randy said pointing at the red and green striped bowling shoes on her feet. "I picked them up at this vintage clothing store in the East Village. I didn't even realize they were bowling shoes at the time, and I used to wear them everywhere."

"Are you kidding?" Sabs asked, giggling. "You walked around in red and green striped shoes?"

"She wears tiger striped sneakers," Katie reminded her, laughing, too. "Why wouldn't she wear red and green bowling shoes?"

"Could you see me in penny loafers?" Randy asked, and we all burst out laughing. Randy is definitely not the penny loafer type.

When we all had our shoes on, we walked over to see which lane we could use. Suddenly, we heard Sam calling out to us.

"Hey, you guys! Over here! We saved you a lane!"

Sabs groaned. "Oh, no! Now we won't even have a chance to warm up without them watching us."

Randy looked over at me. "Don't worry about it, Al. It's no big thing," she said quietly.

I smiled at her. Randy never seems to get nervous about anything, but she almost always notices when I'm nervous. And she usually knows what to say to make me feel better.

"Have you guys been here long?" Katie asked when we walked over to Sam and his friends. They were sitting in front of lanes seventeen and eighteen.

"Oh, we just got here," Sam said with a grin. "We've been waiting for you. We would have started warming up, but we didn't want to have an unfair advantage."

"Oh, come on, Wells," Nick Robbins said, grinning so that his dimples showed. "We've had a warm-up game so they should get one, too."

"Sam Wells!" Sabrina exclaimed, putting her hands on her hips and trying to look angry. "I can't believe you were trying to cheat like that."

"That's just because he's afraid that we're

going to beat him," Katie said. "And we will!"

"Come on, Al," Randy said. "I'll help you pick a ball." She led me over to a long rack of bowling balls. I couldn't believe how many there were to choose from. There were more than a hundred bowling balls on the rack, I was sure.

"Why are there so many balls?" I asked Randy. "There aren't enough lanes for that many people to bowl at the same time."

"They're all different weights," Randy explained to me. "Some people like bowling with a light ball, and some people like heavy balls instead. Try this," she added, handing me a red ball with the number ten on it.

We went back to lane eighteen, where Sabs and Katie were waiting with their balls.

"You go first," Randy told me, sitting down in one of the chairs the boys had saved for us.

"I don't even know what to do," I protested.

"I'll go first," Katie volunteered. "Al, watch me. I'll try and show you."

"Great," I said happily.

"Go, Katie!" Sabs called as Katie stepped up to the line.

I watched as Katie took a position near the

center of the lane, looked down at the row of pins, took a couple of steps forward, and swung her arm back. Then the ball rolled straight down the lane. Suddenly there was a loud crash and all ten pins fell to the floor, spinning around on their sides.

"Awesome!" Sabrina exclaimed. "You got a strike! Well, I'm next," Sabs announced, picking up her ball from the little rack in front of us and walking forward.

She stopped at the line, used both hands to bring the ball up to her nose, then took a couple of hopping steps forward. Sabs had one hand under the ball and the other on top, so that when she threw it, she looked as if she was throwing a bucket of water at someone. After she let go, the force of her swing made her turn a complete circle on the slippery wood of the lane. Everybody laughed — including Sabs — but the ball kept rolling, finally knocking down three pins.

"I still have my second roll," Sabs declared, picking up her ball which had been automatically returned to the rack. "I even have a chance at a spare."

"Well, her technique's pretty weird," Katie

said as we watched Sabs' ball roll down the lane and knock down four more pins. "But you have to admit that it works!"

"Seven pins," Sabs said proudly, coming back to sit down. "Just wait until I'm all warmed up. You guys don't have a chance."

"We're nervous already," Sam said, holding up his hand to show us how badly he was shaking.

"Yeah," Jason agreed. "It looks like you guys don't need any more warming up. Let the challenge match begin!"

"Hold it!" Randy said shortly. "You guys had a warm-up game. We get one, too. Besides, Al and I haven't even tried yet."

"Yeah, Al. It's your turn," Katie said. "Just pick up your ball and we'll tell you exactly what to do."

"Okay, Al," Katie said patiently after I had picked up the red ball from the rack. "Just look where you want the ball to go. Then bring your arm straight back and step forward at the same time. Let the weight of the ball pull your arm forward. Then let go when the ball is in front of you."

Keeping Katie's instructions in mind, I tried

to copy the smooth motions she had made earlier. Unfortunately, it didn't quite work.

"All right, Allison! A perfect gutter ball," Greg Loggins announced with a loud obnoxious snicker.

"Shut up, Greg," Randy snapped, glaring at him, her eyes almost black.

"I'd like to see you do better," Katie added.

"Give her a break, Loggins," Nick said. "She's never bowled before."

"That was a good first try," Katie encouraged me. "Go ahead and try again."

"Here goes," I said, trying to sound confident. I looked at the pins in front of me and concentrated. But this time, as my arm came forward, I realized that my thumb was stuck and I couldn't let go of the ball. When it finally flew off my finger, the ball went flying through the air and landed on the lane with a solid *THUNK.*

"Hey, Al, this is *bowling*, not basketball. No dribbling the ball!" Sam teased me.

"You should have told me that earlier," I joked back, watching the ball roll slowly into the left gutter.

"I knew we forgot to tell you something

important," Katie teased, trying not to laugh.

I took my seat next to Randy. "I'll know what to do next time," I said, grinning and watching Randy get up to take her turn. She walked up to the line confidently and bowled smoothly, just like Katie. Her first ball knocked down seven pins, and her second caught the other three, giving Randy a spare. The guys looked impressed, and Katie gave her a high five.

"Hey, look over there," Sabs whispered suddenly, nudging me in the ribs. "It's him! It's him!"

I looked over to where Sabs was pointing, and I think my heart must have skipped a couple of beats. Billy Dixon was standing by the pinball machines. *What's he doing here?*, I thought to myself.

"Allison, it's your turn again," said Randy. I realized that Sabs and Katie had both bowled while I was watching Billy.

"Go for it," Sabrina whispered. "I think he's watching."

"I hope not," I whispered back nervously. I walked forward slowly and picked up my ball. Again, I went through the same motions while keeping my eye on the pins. No sooner had the ball left my hand when it was in the gutter again. I glanced over toward the arcade. Billy was leaning against the wall, looking my way and grinning. I looked away quickly.

I took the ball for my second shot, but it wasn't much better. I was definitely turning out to be the queen of gutter balls.

Walking back to my seat, I took another quick glance at the arcade out of the corner of my eye. But Billy wasn't there anymore. Had he left already? Somehow I felt kind of disappointed.

"Hi, Allison," a low voice said suddenly from behind me. Startled, I turned around. It was Billy!

"Um, hi, Billy," I stammered, feeling all of my friends eyes on me and knowing that they were listening to every word.

"Having fun?" Billy asked, smiling.

"Well," I replied, "this place is great, but I'm not sure I'm cut out for this game."

"Maybe you need a tutor," he said, grinning.

"Maybe I do," I answered, smiling back at him.

I looked around, and noticed that all the

guys were staring at Billy. Greg leaned over and whispered something in Jason's ear, and I saw Jason nod.

"Are you here with all these people?" Billy asked.

"Yeah," I replied. "Do you know any of them?"

"I've seen them around school," he said vaguely

"Are you here with someone?" I asked, not really sure what else to say.

"Uh, not yet," he answered. "I mean, I was supposed to meet my brother here, but he hasn't shown up yet."

Billy stared at me as if he was waiting for me to say something, but I just couldn't think of anything to say. I had never really talked to Billy outside of our tutoring sessions, and I didn't want to talk about tutoring on a Friday night in a bowling alley!

"Hey, Al! It's your turn," Randy called out. Sabs, Katie, Jason, Nick, Greg and Sam were all staring at Billy and me when when I turned around.

"Um, you guys," I began, "this is Billy Dixon."

"Hi, I'm Sabrina," Sabs cut in quickly, waving a little. One thing I can say about Sabs is that she's definitely not shy. Then everyone introduced themselves and Billy mumbled hello to all of them.

"Are we going to get started, or what?" Greg asked obnoxiously as soon as the introductions were over.

"I have another practice turn first," I replied, walking to the rack and picking up my ball. Sabs looked shocked at the way I had spoken to Greg, and I could see Randy hide a grin. I smiled back and stepped up to the lane. Billy walked over and stood right behind me. Having him so close definitely made me nervous, but at the same time, I was really glad that he was there.

"Keep your wrist pointing straight down the center of the lane," Billy instructed me, reaching out and turning my hand a little bit. "Now, do everything just like you did before, but let go of the ball when I tell you to, okay?"

"Okay," I replied quietly. I concentrated on keeping my wrist in the same position as I swung the ball. Suddenly Billy yelled, "Now!" I let go of the ball. I watched it roll smoothly down the lane, knocking over six pins.

"Way to go, Allison!" Sabs yelled excitedly.

"Not bad," Billy commented, grinning. "We make a good team. Now, all we have to do is knock down the other four pins."

"Oh, no," I groaned. But secretly I was feeling great. Finally, I was really bowling! And it was Billy who was helping me. I couldn't figure out which part made me feel better.

"No problem," Billy assured me. "We just have to aim a bit to the right this time."

"No problem," I repeated, picking up my ball. Again, Billy guided my arm. A few seconds later, two more pins had fallen.

"Sorry," Billy said. "I was a little bit off, or we would have gotten all of them."

"Are you kidding?" I asked in surprise. "Those are the only eight pins I've ever knocked down in my life. That was amazing!"

Billy started laughing as we walked back to my seat. "We'll get 'em all next time," he promised.

Next time? That means he's going to stay and help me, I practically sang to myself. And yesterday I had been worried that he wasn't going to talk to me ever again!

"Is everyone ready to start?" Sam asked after

Randy had taken her last practice frame.

"Sure," Randy replied.

"Why don't we keep score for you guys, just in case you want to give yourselves some bonus points when we're not looking?" Katie suggested teasingly.

"Go ahead," Sam said. "You don't have a chance anyway!"

"We'll see," Sabs put in, glaring at her brother. "Katie, why don't you go first? I'll go second," she added.

"I'll go first for our team," Nick said. "Loggins, you go next. Then Jason, and Sam can go last."

"That means I have time to get some fries and a soda," Sam said, standing up and walking toward the snack bar.

"Bring back extra," Sabs called after him.

Nick and Katie picked up their balls to take their first turns. In two frames, Nick scored nine points and Katie scored only seven. I guess she was a little nervous.

Greg and Sabs went next. As usual, Sabs used her "bucket of water" throw and ended up turning herself completely around in a circle. Greg was laughing hysterically — until all ten pins fell down!

"A strike!" Katie yelled, running forward to give Sabs a hug.

"Way to go, Sabs!" Nick exclaimed.

"Nick! Quit cheering for the other side!" Greg scolded him angrily, before starting his own turn. His first frame was a gutter ball. Greg looked so mad that none of us could help laughing. His second try was only a little bit better, and he ended up with just two points.

When my turn came, Billy helped me again, turning my wrist and telling me when to let go. I scored nine points total and Sabs started jumping up and down with excitement. Jason only scored eight, which meant that we had definitely taken the lead. When Sam came back, carrying four orders of fries, he couldn't believe the score.

"He's not going to help her the whole time, is he?" Greg asked, looking pointedly at Billy.

"Hey, she's never bowled before," Nick replied. "Don't worry about it."

Greg didn't answer, but I knew he wasn't very happy about Billy helping me out, especially since we were winning.

By the end of the fifth frame, we were ahead

by twelve points. The guys were starting to look nervous, but everyone was laughing and having fun — including me.

After the seventh frame, the guys had tied the score. But by the next frame Greg had messed up again, scoring only five points while Sabs got eight, so we were ahead three when my turn came. Billy, as usual, walked up to the line with me. Greg glared at him fiercely.

"Enough is enough!" Greg exclaimed. "Allison doesn't need help anymore!"

I turned around and looked at Greg.

"I thought it was no problem," Randy said loudly.

"Yeah, well it bothers me now," Greg retorted loudly, his arms crossed over his chest.

"Chill, Loggins," Sam said. "What's the big deal? It's only a game."

"And anyway," Greg continued, ignoring Sam. "I don't remember asking Billy Dixon to be here. He's nothing but trouble — big trouble!"

I stared at Greg in disbelief. How could he say something like that about Billy? What had Billy done to him? I had been annoyed with Greg before, but now he was making me really angry. I looked at Billy. His hands were clenched into fists and his blue-grey eyes were flashing. I had to do something before Billy got too upset.

"I'm not surprised that he cheats, either," Greg went on.

"Billy would *never* cheat," I said firmly. "If anybody cheats here, it's you," I added, stepping forward and pointing a finger at Greg. I noticed that my finger was shaking, so I stuck my hands down by my sides.

"What are you talking about?" Greg demanded, scowling at me.

"I mean, there are rules you're supposed to follow when you bowl and they're posted right there," I told him, pointing to the list of rules on the wall above the main desk. "Rule number seven says that bowlers can be disqualified for stepping over the front line. And you've stepped over the line almost every frame! If that isn't cheating then I don't know what is."

Billy took a step toward Greg, his blue eyes flashing.

"Uh, oh," Sabs muttered behind me.

I turned around and saw the manager walking toward us. He must have heard Greg yelling. I didn't want Billy to get into trouble so I stepped between Billy and Greg.

"It's not worth it, Billy," I said softly. Then I spun around and walked up to the lane. I had to show Greg Loggings — and all of them for that matter, that I could bowl without Billy's help. Nobody said anything as I looked down the lane towards the pins and turned my wrist until it felt right. I took a step and swung the ball. It rolled smoothly right up the center, knocking down all ten pins with a huge *CRASH*. A strike! My first strike!

I could hear Katie, Sabs and Randy clapping and cheering, but the person whose face I most wanted to see was Billy's. I wanted to thank him for being such a great tutor. But when I turned around, he was gone.

Chapter Seven

I went to school early on Monday to talk to Ms. Staats about Billy. I had been thinking about him all weekend, wondering if he was still upset about how Greg had acted.

Ms. Staats agreed that Billy should be tested as soon as possible. Later, during English, she called me up to her desk to tell me that she had made an appointment for Billy with a reading specialist for Tuesday after school. It was really important to me that I be the person to tell Billy, and she agreed.

"Hey, Al," Sabs said as soon as we sat down in the cafeteria during lunch. "What was Ms. Staats talking to you about? Was it the tutoring program?

"Sort of," I replied. "I was talking to her about Billy. Remember how I told you that Billy came over to my house to study last Thursday? Well, Charlie asked him to read a story while he was there. I noticed that Billy kept making mistakes and I couldn't figure it out." I took a sip of my milk and then explained what my mother had told me. "So, now, Billy has to take diagnostic reading exams to find out whether or not he has a reading disorder."

Katie whistled. "Wow! I can't imagine being in seventh grade and not knowing how to read!" she exclaimed. "What does a reading disorder do to you?"

"There are a lot of different disorders," I answered. "But I think Billy has dyslexia. There are all kinds of dyslexia, but basically it means there's kind of a mix-up in the way he sees words."

"That's wild," Randy commented. "So what can he do to get over it?"

"I don't really know much about it yet," I replied. "But if Billy actually does have a reading disorder, then he'll probably start working with a reading specialist. My mother told me that they would have to retrain him to read."

"Will you still get to be his tutor?" Katie asked.

"I don't know," I replied. For some reason, I felt my cheeks grow hot. It never occurred to me that I wouldn't continue being Billy's tutor.

Sabrina started giggling. "You will if Billy has anything to say about it!" she said.

"What do you mean?" I asked, looking at her in confusion.

"I think Billy has a major crush on you!" Sabs announced.

I stared at Sabrina, my jaw falling open in surprise.

She nodded, smiling. "Why else would he have spent so much time helping you at the bowling alley on Friday?"

"I don't think he ever took his eyes off of you," Katie teased.

I was so shocked that I didn't know what to think, let alone say. Could Billy actually have a crush on *me*?

"It's so romantic," Sabs gushed. "Allison helps Billy discover that he's actually a total genius underneath, only all this time he's had a reading disorder that nobody knew about."

She sighed dramatically. "It's like this great movie I saw once about this incredibly gorgeous wounded soldier who totally fell in love with the woman who nursed him back to health. She thought at first that he only loved her because she had helped him to walk again, but he finally convinced her that he really loved her, and they ended up getting married and living happily ever after."

Randy was looking at Sabs and shaking her head. "Love stories," she commented sadly. "They turn your brain to mush."

Katie and I looked at each other and started laughing. But then I started thinking about what Sabrina had just said, and I didn't feel like laughing anymore. If Billy really did have a crush on me — and I found it extremely difficult to believe that he did — it was probably only because I was his tutor.

"So, what does Billy think about all of this?" Katie asked as soon as she had caught her breath. "I don't know," I confessed. "He doesn't know yet."

"Whoa!" Randy exclaimed. "Don't you think Billy's going to be a little bit upset?"

"Maybe one of the teachers should tell him," Katie put in, her blue eyes serious.

"No, Ms. Staats and I decided that it would be better if I told him," I replied, shaking my head. "Besides, I *want* to do it." I knew, the way I just know things sometimes, that it was my responsibility and it was important for me to do it personally.

Randy stared hard at me and ran a hand quickly through her spiked bangs.

"Wow, Al. I think you're really, really brave," Sabrina said solemnly.

"I think you should have a teacher tell him," Katie said. "But if you really want to do it yourself, now's your chance." She pointed over Sabrina's head. I looked in that direction and saw Billy standing beside a table with his lunch tray in his hands. He was dressed in a pair of tan pants, with a white mock turtleneck, work boots and his brown leather jacket. Our eyes met across the lunchroom, and I could see him start to smile. His eyes crinkled in the corners the way they did when he laughed. I smiled back as I watched him sit down.

"Look!" Sabrina called, craning her neck in order to see Billy. "There's an empty seat right across from him, Al. Why don't you go talk to him now?"

"I don't know," I said hesitantly. Even though I wanted to talk to Billy, I didn't think that now was the right time. I didn't have all my thoughts in order yet.

"Oh, go on," Sabs said persuasively. "I think you should go over and sit with him. He probably wants you to come over and talk to him anyway."

"Sabs is right about this one," Randy agreed. "He keeps looking over here. And you know how guys are — he would never make the first move and come over here."

"Just make sure you tell us absolutely every word he says," Sabs added.

I looked at my three best friends, all watching me expectantly. I really didn't want to talk to Billy now, in a cafeteria full of people. My instincts told me that it wouldn't be the right thing to do, but with all of them staring at me and looking so concerned, I started thinking that maybe they were right. I stood up slowly and walked over to the table where Billy was sitting, thinking furiously about what I wanted to say. When I got there, Billy looked up and grinned at me.

"Hi, Allison," he said quietly.

"Hi, Billy," I replied. "Um, is it okay if I sit down?"

Billy's grin got wider and his eyes lit up. I had never seen them so blue before. "Sure.

What's up?"

I sank down into the seat across from him. "Well, there's something I wanted to talk to you about," I began, twisting my hands nervously in my lap. My tongue felt as if it was covered with glue, and I couldn't look Billy in the face.

"Me, too," Billy said, leaning toward me. "But you go ahead first."

"First of all, I wanted to apologize for the way Greg Loggins acted at the bowling alley, and I wanted to thank you for helping me out with my bowling," I said quickly.

"No problem," Billy replied with a smile. "It was no big deal.

Then I cleared my throat. "The other thing I wanted to talk about is our tutoring sessions," I told him.

"Oh," Billy said, his grin disappearing. "What about them?"

"Nothing bad," I reassured him quickly. "Actually, I don't even know why you need a tutor for most things. You're much better at math then I am and you have an incredible memory." I was babbling, but I didn't know how to stop myself.

"What are you saying?" he asked after I had

been silent for a moment.

I gulped. "Well, there is one thing that you still have problems with," I said hesitantly, hunting for the right words.

"What?" Billy asked. He had this defiant kind of look on his face as if he was daring me to say what I had to say. I took a deep breath. It was now or never. "Reading," I finally blurted out.

Billy sat back, looked over at the people sitting next to us, and then looked back at me with a scowl. "I already told you. I hate reading," he said, biting the words off, his like blue steel.

"When you were helping Charlie the other day, I noticed a kind of pattern," I continued, determined to finish what I had started.

"Yeah? So I made a couple of mistakes. So what?" Billy retorted, his eyes sparking so that they looked like blue fire.

"So, I did a little research, and I talked to Ms. Staats. Billy, we think you might have a reading disorder," I finished in a rush.

Billy stared at me, his face getting red. I thought for sure he was going to start yelling, but he didn't. He just sat there for a few seconds without saying a word.

"I thought you were different," he said slowly. "But you're not. You think I'm stupid just like everybody else does."

"No!" I cried. How could he have misunderstood me so badly? "That's not true. I know you're smart!" I insisted. "That's why I asked Ms. Staats to have you tested. She has set up an appointment for you tomorrow. If you really have a reading disorder, there are people who can help you learn to read better."

Billy stood up suddenly. He towered over me, his fists clenched at his sides. "I don't need any help, Allison Cloud," he told me. "Not yours, not anybody's. And I don't need any tests, either. So you can tell Ms. Staats to forget it."

He turned around and started to walk away, then turned back to look at me one more time. "I was doing just fine until you came along and stuck your nose in my business," he added, glaring at me. "I hope you're happy now." With that, he stalked away.

I sat there for a moment, staring after Billy. If only I had followed my instincts! If I had waited until I had the chance to really think about what I was going to say, maybe I wouldn't have hurt Billy so badly. Now I had ruined everything!

"Al?" Randy said softly. I looked up. She was standing next to the table.

"He didn't take it too well, huh?" she asked, straddling the chair where Billy had just been sitting.

I shook my head miserably.

"What happened?" Randy questioned.

"I did everything wrong," I told her. "I should have waited until I knew exactly what I wanted to say. Now he thinks that I think he's stupid."

Randy was quiet for a second. "So, what are you going to do about it?" she finally asked, looking directly into my eyes.

"Do?" I asked dully, shrugging my shoulders. "What can I do? I can't force him to take the test." I felt totally defeated. Billy would probably never learn to read.

"So you're just going to let him beat you," Randy said.

I stared at her in surprise. What did she mean? "That's easy for you to say," I blurted out. She had no idea how badly I felt about hurting Billy.

"You're supposed to be the tutor," Randy continued slowly. "You can't just give up on him like that. You've got to make him understand how important it is that he keep his appointment with the reading specialist. It's up to you, Al."

I started to say something and then I thought for a second about what Randy had said.

"You're right, Ran," I suddenly said, sitting up in my chair. "I can't just give up on him." That was the problem in the first place. One of the reasons that he had spent seven years in school without learning to read was that everyone else had done just that — give up.

"I know that Billy can learn to read, and I'm going to prove it to him," I continued. "I'm going to go over to his house after school and make him listen to me!" I exclaimed.

Chapter Eight

At four o'clock that afternoon, I was standing outside the front door at 312 Callahan Drive
trying to get the courage up to knock. I took a
deep breath and stared at Billy's house. It was
dingy gray and the paint was peeling. I reached
out and rang the doorbell, but there was no
sound from within. Taking a step forward on
the sagging front porch, I reached for the screen
door handle. As I opened it, I noticed a long rip
along the bottom half of the screen. Knocking
quickly, I stepped back and waited, trying to
think of what I was going to say. Somehow I
had to talk Billy into taking that test.

After a moment, the door opened.

"Yeah?" an older, blond-haired boy asked,
sounding bored. I figured that he must be Tom,
Billy's 18-year-old brother.

I cleared my throat. "Is Billy home?" I asked
in a small voice. I wasn't afraid of Tom, or any-

thing, but Sabs had told me that he had dropped out of high school and was working as a mechanic. I had never met a high school dropout before.

"Yeah," Tom said again, looking at me with new interest. "Do I know you?"

"No," I said quickly. "I'm Billy's tutor."

"Oh," he answered, as if that explained something. "He's downstairs in the basement. I've got to run."

I really would have rather talked to Billy on the porch than in the house. Randy is always teasing me because I like to be outside in open spaces instead of inside in small rooms. I hate rooms with no windows.

Tom held open the screen door and stepped back. I took a deep breath and walked into the house. "The second door on the right in the kitchen," he called over his shoulder as he walked off across the lawn that I noticed badly needed cutting.

Feeling a little lost, I looked around at the front hall. The carpet was dirty and threadbare and there were shoes and boots lying all over the hall. I suddenly remembered what Sabs had said about Billy's mother having died.

"Billy," I called hesitantly. I could feel the floor vibrating with music coming from the basement. There was no way Billy could hear me. I had no choice. I was going to have to go down there.

Stepping gingerly around the shoes, I walked forward down the hall. The living room was off to the left. Peering into it, I saw that the room was in worse shape than the front hall. It looked as if it hadn't been cleaned in years. Someone had left the television on with the sound turned down. I walked through the room and bumped into the coffee table. I knocked over two empty pop cans and jostled several dirty plates. Newspapers and magazines were lying everywhere.

I quickly walked into the kitchen. The sink was piled with dirty dishes. When I stepped closer to the table, my feet crunched on some spilled sugar. My fingers itched to pick up a sponge and clean up the whole mess. Instead, I turned determinedly toward the basement door. My mission was really clear now. I had to find Billy and get him to take that test.

I knocked on the door, but the heavy metal music was really loud and no one answered. I

knocked a second time, I knew that Billy probably couldn't hear me over all that noise, but I
kept my fingers crossed anyway. I really didn't
want to go down to the basement.

I knocked loudly a third time, but no still no
one came to the door so I took another breath
and pushed it open.

"Billy," I called again, wishing he would
hear me. When I got to the bottom of the stairs,
I jumped in surprise. Billy wasn't alone. There
were six or seven boys there, and they all
looked older than me. They were dressed alike
in T-shirts and ripped-up jeans. I blinked in
confusion. I didn't see Billy anywhere.

A boy who was playing cards at a folding
table near the door suddenly looked up. His
hazel eyes widened in surprise as they met
mine. Flipping his long brown hair over his
shoulder, he reached out and shut off the
stereo. The silence was deafening.

Suddenly, I noticed Billy standing in the corner by the pool table. He had a cue stick in his
hand and a completely shocked expression on
his face.

"Allison?" he asked, taking a step forward.
"What are you doing here?"

I sighed in relief. Even though Billy looked surprised, he was grinning at me. I grinned back.

"Allison?" another boy asked, looking at me with interest. He had to be Billy's brother, Kevin. They looked so much alike that if I hadn't known better, I would have sworn they were twins. "How ya' doing?"

"My name is Kevin," Billy's brother said, standing up and offering me his chair. "Are you a friend of Billy's?"

"She's my tutor," Billy practically spat out, knocking his pool stick against the floor.

Walking over to Kevin's chair, I glanced back at Billy, hoping he'd rescue me. But he was scowling fiercely. What had I done, I wondered, that Billy was suddenly looking so mad?

I smiled a little hesitantly at him. I knew Kevin was in high school. I looked back over at Billy helplessly. I really wanted to talk to him. I just didn't know how to begin with all of these boys around.

"Are you thirsty?" a black-haired boy asked, getting up from the folding table. "Would you like a soda?"

I didn't know what to say, so I just nodded.

"Oh, so, Billy, she's not your girlfriend or anything?" the black-haired boy asked, placing a bottle of soda in front of me.

"Oh, no," he answered, narrowing his eyes at me. "No way. Definitely not." He lay the pool stick down on the table and crossed his arms.

Why was he being like this? He could at least say we were friends. Sabs was totally wrong about Billy. He definitely didn't like me at all. In fact, at that moment, he looked as if he hated me.

I could feel tears welling up and I blinked furiously trying to keep them back.

"I'm Joe," the black-haired boy said, sitting down across from me. "And this is D. J. and Eric," he went on, gesturing to the other boys at the table. Someone coughed loudly by the pool table. "Oh, and that's Psycho playing pool with Billy back there, and this is Ricky," Joe finished, gesturing to a boy lounging on an olive green sofa.

I murmured hello to all of them and took a sip of soda. I couldn't wait to get out of there. I felt kind of like a bird I wrote a poem about once. The bird was stuck in a glass cube and even though it could see all the trees and grass and everything, it couldn't get out of its cube. It just kept flying into the glass walls and falling to the ground. Anyway, I kind of had the same trapped sensation now. I just wanted to be outside.

"So, Allison, what grade are you in?" D. J. asked, leaning forward a little.

"Seventh," Billy answered for me. I looked at him and he glared back.

"Billy, we're talking to Allison here," Joe tossed over his shoulder. "Why don't you just go back to your pool game, okay?"

Billy looked as if he were going to say something else, but instead whipped around and snatched the stick off the table. "Come on, Psycho," he spat out. "What are you waiting for?"

Psycho shrugged, winked at me, and then turned back to the game.

"Don't mind my little brother, Allison," Kevin said, pulling up an old rattan stool next to me. "He can get really moody."

"Definitely," Ricky put in from the couch, brushing a lock of dirty blond hair out of his eyes. "I think the dude's unstable."

"So, you're in seventh grade, huh?" Eric asked, shuffling the cards. "Is that hag Munson still teaching?"

I nodded, even though I didn't think Miss Munson was a hag.

"I had her in eighth grade. She was the worst," Joe agreed.

"Listen, Allison," D. J. began, but he was cut off.

"There's this ninth grade dance next Friday," Joe interrupted.

"Yeah," Kevin added, "do you want to go?"

They all kind of leaned forward, looking at me. I brushed my braid back over my shoulder and studied my pop bottle. I didn't know what to do or say. I had never been asked out by a boy at all before — let alone a whole group of them.

Suddenly, a loud bang reverberated through the basement. I practically jumped out of my seat.

"Dude!" Pyscho yelled, from under the pool table. "Watch what you're doing! You almost took off my head!"

Billy glared at him and stalked over to the the other side of the table. He reached down and picked up a pool ball off the carpet.

"Unstable," Ricky repeated from the couch.

I took the opportunity to stand up. I really had to get out of there. I could feel Billy's hostility from across the room. Sabs is always saying that I have a sixth sense about people's feelings. But I didn't need a sixth sense to know that Billy hated me. At this point, I just wanted to go home.

"Where are you going?" Joe asked, as he turned away from Billy. "You're not leaving, are you?" He sounded really disappointed.

"I have to go home to help my mother with dinner," I said.

"Oh, no!" Kevin exclaimed. "Do you really have to leave?"

I couldn't believe how upset these guys were that I had to go home. There was only one I cared about though, and Billy wouldn't even meet my eyes.

I nodded. "I'm sorry, but I have got to get home."

I inched toward the stairs.

"Well, I hope we see you around, Allison," D. J. said.

I ran up the basement stairs and stood in the

kitchen for a moment trying to get my bearings. Hearing footsteps behind me, I took off for the front door. But the person behind me reached the kitchen just as I put my hand on the doorknob. I pulled open the door and fumbled with the catch on the screen for a moment. Finally, I released it. I actually had the door open and was about to step out onto the porch, when an arm reached around me and pulled the screen door shut.

I spun around startled, and found myself looking straight into Billy's blue-grey eyes. They were the color of steel.

"Why are you in such a rush, Allison?" Billy asked sarcastically.

The tears that had been threatening earlier returned. I knew I was going to start crying at any second, and I was definitely not going to do it in front of Billy Dixon.

"Let me go," I said softly, blinking furiously.

"Come on, Allison," Billy went on. "Don't you want to go back down and talk to your brand new friends? Don't let me stop you."

"What are you talking about?" I asked him, confused.

Billy wasn't making any sense. Why in the

world would I want to keep talking to his brother and their friends? I didn't even know any of them.

"*Well?*" he asked snidely.

It was that one word that did it. I couldn't help it. Billy was being so mean to me and I really didn't understand why. I started crying. Not a lot, but a few tears rolled down my cheeks and I couldn't stop them. And I couldn't look at Billy any more. Since I didn't want him to see, I stared at the floor and watched as my tears hit the carpet by Billy's feet.

Billy didn't say anything for a few minutes. Then he whispered one word, "Allison."

He put his hand under my chin and raised my head. I noticed that his eyes were soft now, like a cloudy sky. Staring into them for a moment, I forgot everything — including my need to get out of his house. Then it all came back in a rush. I jerked my head away, pushed open the screen door, and practically jumped off the porch.

"Just leave me alone," I called out over my shoulder. I didn't slow down even though I heard Billy calling my name over and over as I ran down the street.

Chapter Nine

Billy calls Allison

BILLY: Hello? May I speak to Allison
           please?

ALLISON: Speaking.

BILLY: Allison, this is Billy.

(There is a long pause.)

BILLY: Don't hang up, Allison. I just
           called because I wanted to apolo-
           gize for what happened yesterday.
           I couldn't figure out why you
           came by my house. I'm sorry I
           was so mean to you.

ALLISON: You really were, Billy.

BILLY: I know. But I thought you were
           flirting with my brother and his
           friends. And then I realized that
           you would never do that. You just
           don't do stuff like that.

ALLISON: Flirt with your brother?

BILLY: I know it sounds ridiculous. I'm
            sorry. I keep saying that, don't I?
            (He pauses for a moment.) I
            guess I was a little jealous.

ALLISON: Jealous? What are you talking
            about?

BILLY: Well . . . I . . . uh . . . I didn't want
            you to go out with my brother or
            any of my friends.

ALLISON: I wasn't going to go out with any
            of them!

BILLY: I know, I know. Listen, would you
            . . . would you . . . uh . . . wouldy-
            ougotothemoviewithme?

ALLISON: What?

BILLY: Would you go to the movie with
            me? Friday night at school?

ALLISON: Uh . . . .

BILLY: I didn't think so. Well, anyway, I
            am sorry. I'll see you in school.

ALLISON: NO! I mean, wait, Billy. Yes. Yes,
            I'll go to the movie with you. I'd
            love to go to the movie with you.

BILLY: You would?

ALLISON: Yes, I would. And about those
            tests . . . (Billy laughs.)

BILLY:	You just can't give that tutor stuff up, huh? Well, I thought about what you said, and I went to see Ms. Staats today. And she sent me to the guidance counselor. I'm taking those tests during sixth period tomorrow.
ALLISON:	You are? That's great, Billy!
BILLY:	Well, at least it will get you off my back about them. Right?
ALLISON:	I'm so glad, Billy. This will prove to you that you're not stupid. I always knew you were smart. You are going to let me know how they go, aren't you?
BILLY:	You'll be the first person I tell. Listen, I've got to go. Kevin wants to use the phone. So, we'll talk about the movie later, okay?
ALLISON:	Okay.
BILLY:	See ya tomorrow at school. 'Night, Allison.
ALLISON:	Goodnight Billy.

Allison calls Randy

RANDY:	Hey, Al. What's up?

ALLISON: Hi, Randy. Listen, remember I told you how Billy was acting yesterday at his house . . . .

RANDY: Yeah, he's such a jerk. I can't believe I ever thought he was cool.

ALLISON: He called me to apologize, Randy! He said he acted like that because he was jealous.

RANDY: Jealous?

ALLISON: Yes, can you believe it? Billy told me that he thought I was flirting with his brother —

RANDY: Flirting?! You!? I mean, nothing personal, Al, but you're not really the flirtatious type.

ALLISON: *(giggling)* I know what you mean Randy. But listen, that's not all he said.

RANDY: It's not? What else did he say?

ALLISON: He asked me to the movie on Friday.

RANDY: He asked you to the movie? Al, you've got a date!

ALLISON: Yes, Randy. I know I have a date with Billy Dixon on Friday. Oh, no! Randy what am I going to do? I have a date with Billy Dixon in three days! I've never been on a date before. How am I supposed to act? What am I supposed to do? What if I don't have anything to say? What if we go the whole night without talking to each other? What am I going to do? I have to call him and tell him I can't go with him . . .

RANDY: ALLISON! Get a grip. You're going to be fine. We've got three whole days to get you ready for this date. Don't worry about it.

ALLISON: But, Randy —

RANDY: No buts, Al. We're going to make sure that you are totally ready for this date. I'd better call Sabrina now.

ALLISON: But, Randy —

RANDY: Al, that's what friends are for. Don't worry about it. We'll talk about it tomorrow. *Ciao*!

ALLISON: Good-bye, Randy.

SAM: Yo!

Randy calls Sabrina

RANDY: Sam, it's Randy. What's up?

SAM: Ran! How ya' doin'?

RANDY: Can't complain. Hey, is Sabs there.

SAM: Hold on.

SABRINA: Randy?

RANDY: Sabs, how ya doin'?

SABRINA: Okay. I'm glad you called. I was getting so sick of that math homework. I definitely needed a break.

RANDY: How long have you been working on it?

SABRINA: I don't know. Maybe ten minutes. *(Randy laughs.)*

RANDY: Listen, Sabs. We've got a little emergency here.

SABRINA: What? What happened?

RANDY: Well, Billy Dixon asked Allison to the movie on Friday, and she's really freaking out. I've never seen her like this. We've got to —

SABRINA: Billy asked Allison out? I knew it! I knew he liked her! So, what's the emergency?

RANDY: Let me finish! Like I said, she's really freaking out. She's never been on a date before, and she doesn't know what to do. Al's so bad she was talking about calling Billy and telling him she wasn't going to go with him.

SABRINA: She can't do that! We can't let her do that!

RANDY: Definitely not. So, we've got three days to get her ready for this date. You know how Allison can be. She likes to be totally prepared for things.

SABRINA: So, we've got to help her "study" for her date, right?

RANDY: Right. I knew I could count on you. So we'll talk about it tomorrow, okay?

SABRINA: Definitely. I've already got some ideas . . .

RANDY: Good. Oh, and can you call Katie and fill her in? I've got to get to work on my lab book. *Ciao.*

SABRINA: Bye, Ran.

Sabrina calls Katie

SABRINA: Hi, Katie! You're simply not going

	to believe this, Katie! In fact,I still can't believe it. It is just way too incredible.
KATIE:	SABS! What are you talking about?
SABRINA:	Billy Dixon asked Allison to the movie on Friday.

(There is a long pause.)

KATIE:	Our Allison? Allison Cloud?
SABRINA:	What other Allison do you know? Of course, Allison Cloud. You see, I was right all along. Billy does have a crush on Allison.
KATIE:	This is so cool.
SABRINA:	I know. But here's the thing. Randy said that Al is freaking out because she's never been on a real date. She's afraid that she isn't going to know how to act.
KATIE:	She should just be herself. Why is she worried? It's not as if she doesn't know Billy, or anything.
SABRINA:	A date is different than tutoring someone, Katie. And Randy told her that we'd help her prepare for her date.

KATIE: Prepare for her date? How?

SABRINA: You know, like tell her how to act and what to say and all that.

KATIE: But how are we going to know what she should say? We won't know what Billy's going to say.

SABRINA   Katie! Randy said we should like, you know, help Al "study" for this date.

KATIE: Well, if you guys think so . . .

SABRINA: Definitely. Al's a basket case. We've got to help her calm down.

KATIE: Okay. But I think Al will be fine just being herself.

SABRINA: So, we're supposed to talk about it tomorrow, okay? Listen, I probably should get back to my math. I've only got two problems done.

KATIE: But Sabs, we have to do problems 1-25!

SABRINA: Don't remind me. I'll see you tomorrow, okay? Ta!

KATIE: Bye, Sabs.

Chapter Ten

"So, what happened with Billy's tests, Al?" Randy asked Thursday afternoon. The four of us were up in Sabs' room.

"Oh, yeah," Sabs added from her spot on the floor. "What did happen with that?"

"Well, he took them yesterday," I began, crossing my legs.

"We know that," Katie said, sitting down next to Sabs. "What were the results?"

"Billy tested dyslexic," I explained.

"That's what you thought, wasn't it?" Randy asked, unlacing her black granny boots and dropping them to the floor. "So it's kind of good, right?"

"I guess so," I said slowly. "I mean, it proves that Billy isn't stupid."

"So, what's going to happen now?" Sabs asked curiously. "By the way, does anybody want popcorn? I'm starved."

"I could eat," Randy replied. "Could we get

some juice or something, too?"

"So, Al," Katie prodded, "what's going to happen to Billy?"

"He's got to go to the district reading specialist one period a day," I explained.

"Hey, I'm going down to make popcorn," Sabs interrupted. "You guys want to come?" I was glad she had changed the subject.

We all trooped down two flights of stairs to the Wells' kitchen. Sabrina put the popcorn in the microwave, and we sat down at the kitchen table to wait.

"All right, Al," Sabrina began, putting her elbows on the table and leaning on her hands. "We've got to talk about your date now."

Oh, no, I thought. I had almost forgotten all about my date. I had seen Billy in the library during my free period when he had filled me in about his test. I had felt kind of funny seeing him in person after he had asked me out on the phone, and I think he had felt the same way. He kept looking at his shoes. But then, he said something funny and after I stopped laughing, we were back to normal.

"What time is he coming to pick you up?" Katie asked, opening a bottle of juice. She poured us each a glass. "Or, are you meeting him there?"

"Actually, he's picking me up at six," I replied. "He wants to get something to eat at Fitzie's first."

"He's taking you to dinner?" Sabs asked, squealing. "Al! This is a major date! I'm so excited for you! Billy must really like you!"

I must have looked nervous then — I certainly felt it — because Randy squeezed my shoulder a little. "Don't worry about it, Al," she said soothingly. "You'll have a great time "

"Yeah," Sabrina suddenly said. "It's not like Billy's a stranger or anything, right? It will be fine."

"Besides," Katie put in, "we're going to help you study tonight so you'll be totally prepared."

"That's right," Sabrina agreed. "I think we should start now."

"Now?" I echoed. I wasn't sure that this was such a good idea after all. Who ever heard of "studying" for a date?

"Good idea," Randy said, agreeing. She stood up. "Let's get started."

"What are we going to do?" I asked a little nervously.

"Well," Sabrina began, sounding like a teacher. I fought down the urge to giggle. "We're going to act out your date — with you playing you, of course."

"Act out?" I asked, a little confused.

"Yup," Randy replied. "I'm going to be Billy." She leaned back in her chair, put her stockinged feet on the table and gave me an insolent grin. I couldn't help but laugh. "Katie is going to be our waitress, and Sabs is going to be your coach. Okay?"

I nodded at Randy.

"All right," Sabs directed. "Allison, you sit across from Randy — I mean Billy. Katie why don't you get that popcorn out of the microwave. You can serve that to them."

Katie saluted Sabs. "Yes, sir — I mean, ma'am." Then Sabrina turned back to us. "Now, you guys have just walked into Fitzie's and sat down. What are you going to say now? Al, you start."

I looked at Sabs and then at Randy. I didn't know what to say. Suddenly, I started to panic. I couldn't even start a conversation with Randy/Billy in Sabrina's kitchen. How was I going to be able to handle the real thing?

"Come on, Al," Sabrina coaxed. "Just say something, anything. Don't worry about it so much. Ask him about his interests. Guys love to talk about themselves."

Clearing my throat, I looked at Randy. She nodded slightly. "Uh . . . uh . . . Billy, how'd you do on that math test today?"

"No, no, no!" Sabrina exclaimed, walking around the table. "Don't talk to him about school. I doubt he's really into test scores, even if he is smart. Start again."

I paused, frantically searching for something else to say. "Uh . . . my brother Charlie asked about you "

"Don't you think Billy would have seen Charlie when he came to your house to pick you up?" Katie asked logically, taking a handful of hot popcorn.

"She's got a point there, Al," Randy agreed. "Sorry about that."

"All right, let's start again," Sabrina cut in with a sigh.

"Do you know how to skateboard?" I asked, groping for something about Billy's interests. Randy smiled at me — I guessed that wasn't too bad.

"Well, as a matter of fact —" Randy/Billy began.

"Oh, no!" Sabrina interrupted dramatically. "Don't ask him *that!*"

"Why not?" Randy asked, looking at Sabs. "I think it's a good question."

"Well, of course you do," Sabs retorted, still pacing around the table. "You know how to skateboard. What if Billy doesn't?"

So what if he didn't, I wondered. At least it would start a conversation, wouldn't it? He could tell me he didn't and I could ask him something else.

"Oh," Randy suddenly said. "That's true."

"You know the male ego is an incredible thing," Sabrina replied a little smugly.

"What are you guys talking about?" I asked, totally confused. I just didn't get it.

"Allison, do you know of any guy who will willingly admit that he doesn't know how to do something?" Katie asked, bringing the bowl over to the table.

"Ooohh," I said softly. Boys sometimes do have problems admitting that they can't do something. Look at Billy — he couldn't tell anyone that he didn't know how to read. That definitely made sense to me.

"Okay, okay," Sabrina said, reaching over my shoulder to grab some popcorn. "We'll have to start again. Basically you don't want to ask a question that you don't already know the answer to, Allison. Otherwise you might embarrass him."

Why in the world would I want to ask him a question I already knew the answer to, I wondered. This dating stuff was really complicated.

"Maybe Billy should talk first," Randy suggested. "He seems like that kind of guy."

Sabrina paused in her pacing. "I suppose that's true. All right, Randy — I mean, Billy — why don't you start."

Randy grinned and winked at me. "So, Allison," she began, in a deep voice. "How about those Twins?" I started laughing, and I could hear Katie giggling behind me.

"Come on, guys," Sabrina complained. "Cut it out. This is serious."

"Sorry, Sabs," Randy said, grinning. Randy cleared her throat and took a deep breath. She opened her mouth to say something, but before she could get anything out, her shoulders started shaking and she dissolved in a fit of giggles.

Katie came over and sat down in a chair — she was laughing so hard I don't think she could stand up. I tried to get hold of myself, I didn't want to get Sabs mad. But when I wiped the tears from my eyes, I could see Sabrina sitting on the floor, holding her sides.

And at that moment, Sam, Nick, and Jason burst into the kitchen.

"What's going on?" Nick asked, tossing his jacket on a chair near the back door.

Sam eyed his twin sister skeptically. "Why are you sitting on the floor, Sabs?"

We just laughed harder. The guys looked at each other, shook their heads and left.

"Oh, no," I suddenly said, catching sight of the clock. "I've got to get home for dinner."

"But, Allison, we didn't get to practice!" Sabrina practically wailed.

"Don't worry about it, Sabs," Randy said, trying to calm her down. "Allison will do fine." She turned toward me. "Just be yourself, Al. That's what got him to ask you out in the first place. Don't sweat it."

Randy definitely had a point, I told myself all the way home. Billy wouldn't have asked me out if he didn't like me, and he wouldn't want me to become someone else in the middle of a date. It would be all right. But if that was true, why was I still so nervous?

Chapter Eleven

The next night at five minutes to six, my mother called up the stairs, "Allison! Billy's here!"

I almost jumped. He was early. Taking a deep breath, I wiped my sweaty palms on my thighs and took one last look in the mirror.

Critically, I turned sideways to see my outfit better. I was wearing a red, black and white plaid wool skirt that came to just above my knees and white stockings and black patent leather flats. My mother had given me a new sweater that afternoon, saying something about first dates. The sweater was beautiful. It was just like a plain crewneck, but it was made out of black lambswool. I loved the way it felt as I made sure it was tucked neatly into my skirt. I lifted my eyes to my face. My mother had talked me into leaving my hair down, and it swung neatly down my back. I guessed I looked okay.

"Allison!" my mother called again.

After one last look in the mirror, I grabbed my coat and flew down the stairs. I didn't want to make Billy wait any longer.

Billy was in the living room when I got downstairs. I paused for a moment outside the door and looked inside. Wearing a button down grey-blue shirt that matched his eyes, Billy looked great. His jeans didn't even have holes in them and he was wearing shoes — not sneakers. It kind of made my stomach feel a little funny knowing that Billy had gotten dressed up just for me.

Nooma, my grandmother, was talking to Billy and he looked really interested in what she was saying. Just then, my mother came up behind me.

"He's a very nice young man, Allison," she whispered in my ear.

I gave her a quick hug, took a deep breath and stepped into the living room.

Billy was in the middle of saying something to Nooma but when he caught sight of me his voice just trailed off. Then he stood up and took a step toward toward me. He stopped suddenly as if he remembered that there were other people in the room.

"Have a great time," my mom said, walking us to the front door.

"You look so pretty Allison," Billy said softly as we walked down my front steps. "Really."

Before I could stop myself I replied, "So do you." And we both laughed.

We walked most of the way in silence, but it was a good kind of quiet. I've always thought that if you can be silent with a person for more than ten minutes without thinking you have to say something then that means you're going to be life-long friends. I was glad that I felt like that with Billy.

Fitzie's was really packed when we got there. There wasn't a booth open anywhere.

"Sorry, Allison," Billy whispered in my ear as he stepped into the restaurant behind me. "It doesn't look as if we'll be able to sit by ourselves."

In a weird sort of way, I felt relieved. Now, I wouldn't have to try to make conversation.

"I think my brother and his friends are sitting over there," Billy continued, pointing to the back. "Let's go see if there's room for us at their table."

Billy took my hand and we made our way through the crowd of kids. As we got closer to Kevin's booth, I noticed that Stacy Hansen was sitting in the booth next to his. Her eyes practically drilled holes through me as Billy led me past her. Her gaze stopped at our locked hands and then she glared at me. I could feel her staring even after we had walked past. I straightened my back. I was proud to be there with Billy. I didn't care what Stacy thought. She was probably just jealous.

"Hey, Kevin," Billy said to his brother as he pushed him over on the booth bench to make room for us. "Move over, would you?"

"Yo, Billy," D. J. greeted, looking up from his fries. "Ooohh! What's with the loafers? I don't think I've *ever* seen you in shoes!"

"What's the occasion?" Eric asked, slurping the last of his vanilla milk shake.

Just then, Billy pulled me forward so I was standing at the edge of the table. I smiled hesitantly at Billy's brother and his friends.

"Hey, it's Allison!" Joe exclaimed, a big smile on his face. "How ya' doing, Al?"

Kevin scooted over in the booth to make room for us. He turned toward Billy.

"You didn't tell me you were going out with Allison tonight."

Billy just shrugged and slid into the booth next to his brother. I sat down at the end, and Billy took my hand. Billy glared at all of his friends.

"Oh," Ricky said, moving the ketchup bottle back by the napkin holder. "I get it."

"What?" Joe asked in confusion. Then he looked at Billy and me. "I thought you said she was just your tutor."

"I lied," Billy said simply and then asked for a menu.

D. J. threw a french fry at him and Eric reached over and cuffed his ear. Then everyone was talking at once.

After Billy and I ordered, he put his arm on top of the booth behind me and kind of leaned back. It felt neat to have his arm sort of around me.

Then after what seemed like ten minutes, but was really more like an hour, Billy said we had to go or we'd miss the movie. Grabbing my hand and pulling me to my feet, he threw some money on the table and said good-bye to his friends.

"Good-bye, Allison!" they all called out after us.

Holding hands all the way to school, Billy and I didn't say anything until we got there. It just felt nice to be holding hands.

"Are your friends meeting us here?" he asked, opening the door for me.

I nodded. We went into the gym and bought our tickets. I saw Sabrina waving wildly from a seat near the center of the gym. She pointed to two seats in the row right behind her, and Billy and I walked over and sat down. The entire auditorium was packed with kids. We were just in time for the cartoon.

I couldn't believe how fast the movie went, and I don't even really like horror movies. Of course, it wasn't so bad with Billy's hand in mine. It gave me something to squeeze whenever it got too scary.

Before I knew it, we were on our way home. Randy, Sabrina and Katie said good-bye to us outside school and we walked toward my house alone.

"Your friends are really nice," Billy commented, a little surprised. "I guess I never thought they would be."

"Why not?" I asked him.

Billy took my hand in his, and swinging our arms, we kept walking. "I don't know. I just figured they were like . . . teacher's pets, or something," he said.

"You mean like me?" I asked, grinning in the dark.

"I'm sorry I said that, Allison," he said seriously. "You're not mad, are you?

I laughed. "I was just kidding, Billy."

"Oh," was all he said and we lapsed into silence again.

Much too quickly, we were standing on my front porch. Billy turned to face me, not letting go of my hand.

"I had a really nice time tonight, Allison," he said, his eyes a soft blue-grey color.

"Me, too," I replied, looking down.

"Hey," Billy whispered, cupping my chin with his hand. He pulled my face up so I had to look at him. "You are a really nice person, Allison," he continued, just as softly. "Thank you for everything. " Then he leaned forward and kissed me on the cheek. "Goodnight."

Before I could do or say a single thing, he had turned and walked down the stairs and onto the street. I could hear him whistling as I stood on the porch staring after him. Once, he turned around and waved. I just stood there, my feet glued to the porch. Billy Dixon had kissed me. I touched my cheek. Billy Dixon had kissed me! I couldn't believe it! And I couldn't wait to tell my friends.

Titles in the GIRL TALK series

1 WELCOME TO JUNIOR HIGH!
Introducing the Girl Talk characters, Sabrina Wells, Katie Campbell, Randy Zak, and Allison Cloud. When our four heroines meet and have to plan the first junior high dance of the year, the results are hilarious.

2 FACE-OFF!
Katie Campbell is just plain fed up with being "perfect." But when she decides to join the boys' ice hockey team, she gets more than she bargained for.

3 THE NEW YOU
Allison Cloud is down in the dumps, and her friends decide she needs a makeover, just in time for a real live magazine shoot!

4 REBEL, REBEL
Randy Zak is acting even stranger than usual — could a visit from her cute friend from New York have something to do with it?

5 IT'S ALL IN THE STARS
Sabrina Wells's twin brother, Sam, enlists the aid of the class nerd, Winslow, to play a practical joke on her. The problem is, Winslow takes it seriously!

6 THE GHOST OF EAGLE MOUNTAIN
The girls go camping, only to discover that they're sleeping on the very spot where the Ghost of Eagle Mountain wanders!

LOOK FOR THE GIRL TALK SERIES!
COMING SOON TO A STORE NEAR YOU!

TALK BACK!

TELL US WHAT YOU THINK ABOUT GIRL TALK

Name _____

Address _____

City _____ State _____ Zip _____

Birthday: Day _____ Mo _____ Year _____

Telephone Number (____) _____

1) On a scale of 1 (The Pits) to 5 (The Max), how would you rate Girl Talk?   Circle One:

1   2   3   4   5

2) What do you like most about Girl Talk?

___Characters___Situations___Telephone Talk

Other _____

3) Who is your favorite character?   Circle One:

Sabrina   Katie   Randy
Allison   Stacy   Other

4) Who is your least favorite character?

_____

5) What do you want to read about in Girl Talk?

_____

_____

Send completed form to :
Western Publishing Company, Inc.
1220 Mound Avenue Mail Station #85
Racine, Wisconsin 53404